MEETING LILY

Sarah Woodhouse

PENGUIN BOOKS

PENGUIN BOOKS

Published by the Penguin Group
Penguin Books Ltd, 27 Wrights Lane, London W8 5TZ, England
Penguin Books USA Inc., 375 Hudson Street, New York, New York 10014, USA
Penguin Books Australia Ltd, Ringwood, Victoria, Australia
Penguin Books Canada Ltd, 10 Alcorn Avenue, Toronto, Ontario, Canada M4V 3B2
Penguin Books (NZ) Ltd, 182–190 Wairau Road, Auckland 10, New Zealand

Penguin Books Ltd, Registered Offices: Harmondsworth, Middlesex, England

First published by Michael Joseph 1994
Published in Penguin Books 1995
1 3 5 7 9 10 8 6 4 2

Printed in England by Clays Ltd, St Ives plc

For Brenda

PENGUIN BOOKS

MEETING LILY

Sarah Woodhouse is the author of *A Season of Mists*, *The Indian Widow*, *The Daughter of the Sea*, *The Peacock's Feather*, which won the Romantic Novelists' Association Boots' Romantic Novel of the Year Award in 1989, and *The Native Air*, all of which are historical novels. Her penultimate novel to date, *Enchanted Ground* (Penguin, 1994), was the first to be set in the twentieth century.

She lives on a farm in Norfolk and has two children.

I

MAJOR Baghot died in Nan's best bed.

'How inconsiderate,' said his widow, who had apparently been out in the garden when it happened. 'What a nuisance for you, dear.'

Nan, stricken first by compassion and now by surprise, could only murmur feebly: 'You really mustn't worry about anything. You ought to rest. Dr Fortuno will be here soon.'

'Why rest?' demanded Molly Baghot. 'I shall take my usual walk.'

'To the village?'

'Well, why not?'

Nan imagined Fortuno's old car struggling up the road in a dust cloud, imagined Molly engulfed, indignant, waving a small fist as he passed. '*That* woman,' the doctor would say, scowling. '*That* was the Signora Baghot? But why is she not prostrate?' And he would use the words '*soprafatta dal dolore*', which would sound romantic and highly appropriate to the situation –

though not, evidently, to the Signora Baghot.

What he actually said, quite cheerfully, was, 'Well, what a tragedy for such a beautiful day.'

'Yes,' agreed Nan who felt the power of speech was leaving her. 'I think . . . I hope he died peacefully.'

Although it was early the heat was already intense, every shutter in the house drawn across. She led the way up the wide shallow stairs.

'Mrs Baghot was out in the garden when it happened. Poor Graziella found him.'

'In the garden so early?'

'She was out there yesterday morning at five. And she walks miles. She walks to the village and back after breakfast.'

How English, perhaps he was thinking. 'And now she is disconsolate, the Signora Baghot,' he remarked, savouring the the strange name, so un-Italian.

'I think she's shocked,' said Nan diplomatically. 'So shocked she's pretending it hasn't happened.' But this was most decidedly a lie. At no time had Molly pretended anything. She had received the news calmly and had looked quite unmoved on the face of her dead husband.

In the bedroom Fortuno opened the shutters a little, then switched on the bedside lamp. The body was covered decently with the bedclothes. He pulled them down to reveal the once-florid face, the carefully trimmed moustache.

'*Signora, è morto*. Il Signor Baggotta. *È morto*,' Graziella had whispered in her ear. Nan had thought: The one morning I lie in bed after six and there's a crisis. Then the words had pierced her self-satisfied warmth. '*Morto?*' she had cried, rising from the depths aghast.

It was the first time since the Villa Giulia had been

turned into a small hotel that a guest had died. For two years since Nan had been widowed strangers had come and gone, admiring the views, Pisa, Assisi, Perugia, Maria's cooking. There had been broken bones, stomach upsets, asthmatic attacks, but no deaths.

'How old was he?' asked Fortuno. He had opened his bag but Nan could not see what he was doing. What could one do?

'Seventy-eight.'

'Then no doubt he died of old age in his sleep. He was already dead, probably, when the signora crept out to enjoy the garden.' In the strange mingled light he and Nan looked at each other. Both felt sympathetic and disinterested. The body in the bed meant nothing to either of them, Nan thought guiltily, except as an inconvenience in a day already filled with duties and appointments.

'I'll send for the ambulance.'

'Ambulance?' exclaimed Nan, foolishly astonished.

'A sudden death,' and he shrugged, pulling up the sheet again. 'You're as pale as he is. What are you worrying about?'

She was always pale. The Italian sun did not penetrate beneath her wide-brimmed hats, her respectable, concealing clothes. 'I manage a hotel. I have to look respectable,' she had written to Aunt Dot in England when Aunt Dot had commented unfavourably on some photographs she had sent. 'There's respectable and there's dowdy,' returned Aunt Dot irrepressibly, adding, 'and it's scarcely a proper hotel, is it? It's more a *pensione*.'

'I always prayed that nothing like this would ever happen,' Nan told Fortuno. He was snapping his bag shut. For a moment she saw his face exposed by the lamplight, a handsome serious face, professionally unconcerned.

'Well, there was the baby. Now there's an old man dying. I don't see how you can avoid such things.'

The baby had belonged to Maria's niece Alessandra who, in order to conceal it from her parents, had given birth in Nan's private bathroom. I suppose I coped with that, Nan remembered, after a fashion, and so I shall cope with this.

When she went downstairs she found the young priest Father Michele in the hall. He was standing turning his hat in his hands and looking the picture of adolescent embarrassment. He was too frightened of Maria to venture beyond the foot of the stairs.

'I expect they're Protestants,' Nan told him apologetically. 'But it shouldn't matter. God is God, isn't He?' She longed to give him a solid, practical job to do. He always seemed at a loss, desperate to spread the Word, desperate to justify his vocation. Sometimes she thought he was hardly old enough to be allowed out among the cynical and mischievous. And he was much under the iron thumb of his superior, Father Emilio. It would do no harm, she thought, to let him upstairs to pray over the body while they waited for the ambulance. Molly Baghot had not returned to give or withhold consent. Maria was busy in the kitchen. The Hazelwells were on the terrace in the dappled shade under the vines, oblivious to crisis. Miss Porter and Miss Heber were safely in Assisi.

Half an hour passed.

The ambulance arrived discreetly and drew round the back of the house into the kitchen courtyard. Nan divined Fortuno's delicate hand. Maria said, 'God save us,' as the corpse went past the kitchen table. The ambulance driver said, 'His troubles are well and truly over. No more bills to pay.'

'Perhaps someone should go and find Mrs Baghot,' suggested Father Michele. He said 'Signora Baggotta'.

'I think we could wait a little longer,' Nan told him firmly. He's been speaking to Graziella, she thought. Graziella always turned Baghot into Baggotta. She wondered for a moment how he coped with Graziella, what tone he used with her, what expression. Graziella was only sixteen but already at the peak of her beauty. In ten years she might be slatternly like Maria, putting on weight, but now, incandescent, she would burn through any man's armour, even clerical cloth.

'Something might have happened to her. Would you like me to go?' He was persistent. He was always so eager to be of use. Nan thought: He should have been a missionary.

'I'm sure she's all right. She's very sensible.' But was she? I don't know anything about her, Nan thought. She had a vague impression of a small timid bird-like creature. 'I take good care of my guests,' she often said with justification, but she rarely noticed them as personalities. Even those who stayed a fortnight, three weeks, were nothing more than dim shapes, names in the register. 'I don't get involved,' she might have said if challenged.

'Mrs Baghot's all right,' she repeated. 'A long walk might be just what she needs.'

When Robin had died she had gone down to the meadow and sat under the cherry tree in the long grass and wondered if she would ever be able to move again. It was as if life were leaving her too, seeping away into the baking ground. She had stayed there for an hour with her arms locked round herself defensively, as if by such means she could keep in what little breath remained. Maria had found her at last, had lifted her, stiff and unyielding, and had half carried her to the house, calling out for old Antonio from the vegetable garden, for Pia, for Dr Fortuno, for the Holy Virgin.

It was eleven o'clock.

The house was silent now. Heat enveloped it but did not penetrate. The tall old rooms were cool. On the terrace the Hazelwells dozed, surrounded by discarded guidebooks, maps and postcards. 'Idyllic place, marvellous scenery, Assisi round the corner . . .' began one message home. In the hall Nan's vases of flowers were ghostly in the dimness, great white peonies and roses in romantic profusion.

What a day, Nan thought, leaving her small sitting-room and wandering out of the front door, unsettled. The drive, between myrtles and cypresses, was dusty and deserted. No Molly Baghot tripped through the gates or leaned, weeping, against the stone urns. Alarm fluttered inside Nan and she clutched a hand against her breast as if to quieten it. I'm no good at all this, she thought. I should never have begun it.

She had begun it only because Robin died. He had died in that same bedroom, in that same bed where the Major had lain so stiff and surprised this morning. 'What can I do?' she had asked Umberto Degnare the lawyer, fuddled with grief and chaos. There was no money coming in from anywhere, Robin's means had been as sand, trickling away before her frantic eyes. Degnare, consoling but businesslike, had said encouragingly, 'There is always the villa, signora.' The villa was large and comfortable, was undoubtedly charming. And did not English people love Italy, love charming shabby elegant old houses where they could feel at home instead of loud new defective hotels with rapacious staff? There were three, four spare bedrooms. There was Maria.

6

Maria had once cooked for the Princess Montefarnese in a Venetian palazzo. 'She was very young then,' Nan had protested. Besides, the palazzo had been decrepit, the princess senile.

'A woman like Maria,' insisted Degnare, 'will think nothing of a few well-behaved English guests.'

But would they be well-behaved? Nan said wearily, 'I'd need a licence or something, wouldn't I? Think of the problems.'

'Think of the profit,' said Degnare optimistically.

In only months they had grappled bureaucracy to compliance, had admitted the first guests. How I worked, thought Nan afterwards, amazed. She had worked, schemed, sat hours over columns of figures, and all the time she had felt detached, numb. Against such paralysis physical energy accomplished nothing.

'She has courage,' people said to Degnare.

'More than you think. How she grieves, poor woman,' he would reply solemnly.

Is it grief? Nan wondered. She felt imprisoned behind glass.

She had always expected Robin to die first. He had expected it himself. At odd moments he had referred to death light-heartedly, with the jokiness of a man who, though he thinks the event probable, still hopes to avoid it. He had been more than twenty years older than Nan and his heart and lungs had been affected by gas in the trenches and again by bomb blast in '42. That was why they had come to Italy. 'For Robin's health,' Nan had told Aunt Dot, who had come up to London to say goodbye. For Robin's health – and her own. 'You've never been quite yourself since . . .' said Robin, leaving unspoken everything that should have been said. Did he hope the doctors were wrong, that there would be another baby?

7

'Doctors are often wrong,' Aunt Dot comforted.

'Not in this case. In this case . . .' Nan had begun defiantly, hysterically.

'But look at Mr Huntingdon. They cut off his left leg instead of his right one. How could you put any faith in such men?'

Robin had once said, 'Aunt Dot would be optimistic abandoned on a sandbank surrounded by crocodiles and armed only with a paddle.'

'Then optimists are people with no imagination,' asserted Nan. 'Anyone with imagination would scream and throw down the paddle and try to swim for it.'

'Signora, signora.' Maria waddled round the corner of the house flapping her apron to attract attention. 'Where is Signora Baghot?'

'What is it?' asked Nan.

'*Il telefono.*'

In the hall the peonies had dropped great curling petals on the polished wood. The telephone receiver felt cold and heavy in Nan's hand.

'*Pronto?*'

'I would like to speak to Major Baghot,' an English voice enunciated loudly.

'I'm afraid that's not possible. Could I take a message?' How strange, thought Nan. A phone call for the poor man now he's dead.

The voice modified, grew conciliatory. 'It's rather urgent. My name's Ruddock. I'm Major Baghot's solicitor.'

Should I tell him? wondered Nan.

And: 'Maria,' she called, hurrying to the kitchen. 'Maria, I'm going to drive down to the village to see if I can find Mrs Baghot. I don't think she ought to be out alone any longer.'

8

'She's a little mad,' Maria said, making the appropriate gestures. 'Didn't I tell you so when they arrived? And did you listen? That woman's strange in the head, I said. But no, no, she's only an old lady feeling the Italian sun. Let her walk in the garden. Four, five o'clock in the morning. What does it matter? And now look, the old man dead in bed – your marriage bed, signora – and her carrying on as if nothing had happened.'

'I must go,' murmured Nan and fled.

The Morris started with difficulty. 'It's really very reliable,' she often said at the local garage while they struggled to decoke or regrind or unseize. They had never worked on such a machine. 'Perhaps it's the weather,' they told Nan kindly, for everyone knew it rained most of the time in England and when it stopped raining it was foggy. 'Buy an Italian car, signora. Italian cars love the sun.'

The narrow road to Cittavigile wound first between cypresses. Here Molly Baghot might have lingered to look out across fold upon fold of hills, chequered all shades of green. Here she might have stopped to weep her first tears of widowhood. Or might not.

Nan thought: Where *is* the woman?

She crashed through the gearbox on the bends without the least sympathy for the car. She hated the car. It was fifteen years old, heavy and temperamental, though it had always run more or less sweetly for Robin who had had an affinity with the mechanical. 'We ought to buy something else,' Nan had often said but, 'Oh, she'll do us a year or two yet,' Robin would reply. Even then, Nan suspected, he had been beset by money worries. 'If only he had told me,' she had wailed childishly to Degnare. Another woman might have known without asking, might have taken more notice. 'I was too busy falling in love with Italy,' said Nan to Aunt Dot.

Cittavigile was halfway down the hill, tucked away, instead of being bold and visible on the crown. 'It is a modest village,' said Father Emilio but he looked with covetous eyes, Nan thought, on neighbouring churches, larger and more prominent. The stone walls sent the roar of the Morris's ill-conditioned engine through the quiet streets. It was the lunch hour. Only cats crossed in front of her, and the three-legged dog from the bakery. They're all looking from behind the shutters, thought Nan, prickling as usual with the sense of being observed. In the main square she parked awkwardly, self-conscious, and climbed out.

Molly Baghot was sitting at a table outside the café. Her face was tilted up to the sun, her hat tossed on the ground beside her.

She's certainly strange in the head, thought Nan, but then so was I when Robin died. Exasperation and compassion wrestled in her. For a moment she studied the lined and fragile little face. The lids of the closed eyes were covered by tiny mauve veins. The hair, thin and white, was roughly cut as if a child had been at it. Her dress was a severe grey silk, quite straight, as pre-war as Nan's Morris, but then all her clothes were sensible and featureless as if she simply ordered them by the dozen from the same pattern.

'Mrs Baghot.' Nan reached out a tentative hand. 'Mrs Baghot, I've come to drive you back.'

'But my dear,' and the bright little eyes opened immediately, apparently quite sane, 'my dear, I was looking forward to the walk.'

'It's already after twelve. It's very hot. And the hill . . .'

'*So* shady under the cypresses.'

'. . . And I've asked Maria to do you some lunch. You ought to eat something.'

'Why? I'm really not hungry.'

'No. No, I don't suppose you are. But . . . do come back to the villa. They may call from the hospital.'

'Why should they? They can't revive him, can they?'

Nan felt perspiration trickling between her breasts. She thought how they must look to the curious eyes behind the village shutters: two strange Englishwomen arguing in the sun.

'Please come back.'

'Well, of course, if it worries you so,' and Molly gathered her belongings, tottered straight to the car. 'What a charming old motor. But far too much for you, dear. How can you manage on those wicked bends?'

Nan said nothing and her smile was false. She felt that the situation was absurd, the whole day unreal. She grappled with the car in a silence broken only by the horrible grating of the gears and drove too fast between her own gateposts so that they pulled up at the front door in a haze of dust.

'You look tired out, dear,' remarked Molly sympathetically.

'It's just . . . I'm so sorry about the Major.'

'You shouldn't be,' Molly assured her. 'It's a merciful release.'

But did she mean for the Major – or for herself? wondered Nan.

2

MARIA did not appreciate English sang-froid. When Nan said reasonably. 'Surely there's no need for dinner to be late?' the reply was. 'How can it be helped? This is a house of death.' Temper and indignation seethed in the air.

'That girl,' Maria told her, stabbing a finger. 'That girl drops the plates. She cries.'

'Graziella?' Nan looked suspiciously but saw only luminous young eyes in a pale face – a little paler than usual perhaps but nothing worse. And why should she weep? Not for Major Baghot. A quarrel with Giuseppina then? Shock? Maria shouting?

'Mrs Baghot is having her meal upstairs,' she announced, not to be swept aside by these mysterious undercurrents. She watched Maria's fat competent hands stir and scoop. In the old days, she remembered, the days when she and Robin were newly arrived, she had enjoyed Maria's strength, her undeniable grasp on domestic power. She ran the house better than Nan ever could, who had only run her mother's modern flat and three small rooms in Kensington. The hotel, however, seemed to bring out the worst in her. She regarded the guests as intruders, affronted if they criticized the least thing, if they questioned her cooking, refused a dish. She resented the convent girls who came daily from the village for bed-making and laundry, for the sweeping of floors and polishing of furniture. Once they had managed with Pia, a decayed and conscientious virgin, toothless, devout. Now they suffered Giuseppina and Graziella, women one moment, giggling children the next. 'One eye on the clock, one on the boys,' Maria cried daily, a cauldron of complaint.

'They're only young,' Nan would protest in mitigation when the weekly list of trespass and omission was put in front of her.

'And they're orphans.'

'They're no good,' Maria told her. 'They do half the work they should.'

'What *is* for dinner?' asked Nan, still watching Maria's hands in the pastry. She felt she had lost her grip on the entire day. From the moment Graziella had woken her she had been cast into a void. Usually she could recite the menus for the week but this one . . . *Strascinati? Coniglio?* This one escaped her.

Maria, however, ignored the question. She turned her eyes to the ceiling. 'Is the signora up there going to eat the same as everyone else?'

'I suppose so. She hasn't asked for anything different. Perhaps Graziella could run up and ask. She's in my room, resting.'

'So she should be. First she walks here, then she walks there. Then she runs round the meadow with

Don Emilio. I saw them when I took the chips to the hens. Chatter, chatter. And he was panting to keep up.'

'Do you mean scraps? I think it's shock,' said Nan. She seemed to keep repeating this as if she might somehow make it true.

'*Certo.* Shock. But she smiles!' Maria affected a look of horror. 'She smiles and the old man not buried, not cold!'

'I'm sure he's cold by now. Who knows what she's really feeling? There might be an inquest.'

'*Inchiesta? Inchiesta?* As if he was murdered?'

'Sudden death.'

'I knew it,' said Maria. 'I knew there would be trouble. And afterwards, where is he to rest? Not in the village. He's not a Catholic.'

'He might have been.'

'There are none in England. England is full of heretics. Don Emilio told me so.'

Distantly Nan heard the telephone. It would be Dr Fortuno perhaps or perhaps the bigoted Father Emilio who considered England to be practically a pagan outpost. There would be questions to which she must give intelligent answers. There would be arrangements to make. It reminded her of when Robin had died.

It reminded her of something else.

'Mrs Baghot, your solicitor called. I'm so sorry, I forgot all about it. He asked if you could get in touch as soon as possible. I didn't ... I didn't mention the Major.'

'I don't have a solicitor,' said Molly smugly. She was lying on the day bed in Nan's dressing-room. 'Well, we can hardly ask her to lie down on the bed where her husband died, can we?' Nan had remarked to Maria.

'The Major's solicitor then. Mr Ruddock.'

'Never heard of him.'

'But . . .'

'And you must call me Molly, nothing but Molly. I won't answer to Baghot.'

'I think you should ring him at once.'

'Why should I?'

'Please, Molly.'

But in the hall Nan had to stand over her while the exasperating business of getting through to England was going on. They had found Ruddock's number in the Major's pocket book which lay with his keys and pipe and other pitiful oddments on Nan's dressing-table. 'I don't want them,' said Molly, recoiling. 'You keep them, dear, if you want.'

Now: 'There's no one there,' she announced triumphantly, handing back the receiver.

'*Pronto*,' said Nan briskly. A tired voice explained again that there were no free lines.

'I'm afraid it's often like this,' Nan told Molly. 'Let's hope it wasn't anything serious. But . . .' She hesitated. All day words had failed her. 'But I think you ought to tell him about the Major straight away.'

Molly had lifted her head suddenly, like a small dog to an interesting scent. Dinner perhaps?

'What, dear? What about the Major?'

Nan took a steadying breath. 'That he died last night.'

'Oh, but he's been dead for years,' said Molly.

'She's quite mad,' Nan confided to Fortuno when he came in to see her after dinner. 'First she's never heard of Ruddock, then she says the Major's been dead for years. Is it shock?'

'Perhaps.' He was looking her over, a pitiless professional scrutiny. 'But how are *you*?'

'I feel exhausted.'

Her face never stood up well to crisis. Her skin seemed to become taut and transparent with distress and her blue eyes appeared enormous, bruised and tragic. Only her hair remained untouched, bronze, spilling pins. 'I'm going mousy with age,' she had told Robin shortly before he died but he had only said, 'How absurd you are.' 'There's grey in it,' she had replied, equally absurdly, to some compliment of Fortuno's. She was always self-conscious when admired.

'There's no need to worry about the Major,' he told her now. 'Natural causes. Nothing more sinister.' He spoke brusquely, as to a fidgeting child. She was not a child, she was thirty-six. She looked a little resentful at his tone. Thirty-six and married seven years to a man much older than herself. There had been one child who died. Mentally he recounted these facts while staring at the freckles on her cheekbones and the bridge of her nose. He found her remote, irritating, attractive. He had tried for years to treat her with as much indifference as she treated him.

'What about the funeral?' she was saying.

'Oh, Mrs Baghot will take him back to England.' He spoke as if the Major were ordinary baggage, an extra suitcase.

'I'm sure she won't.'

'Is it your concern what she does with him?'

'Of course it is. I can't leave the poor woman adrift in a strange country. Think of the forms she'll have to fill in . . .'

Fortuno frowned and came to feel her pulse. 'Go to bed early,' he commanded. 'Forget the Major till to-morrow.'

'How can I?' She drew back a little. He always discon-

16

certed her close to, reminding her of young men she might have loved, muscular and athletic. His fingers were slender and hard and she could see the dark hairs springing at the wrist where the brown skin contrasted so admirably with his white cuff.

'I'll go up to Mrs Baghot,' he told her. 'Will you take me or shall I call Maria?'

'No, not Maria.' Maria was still in the ebb of passion.

On the stairs Fortuno held Nan's elbow once or twice as if self-confessed exhaustion made her an old woman. It means nothing, she told herself. The Italians are a tactile nation. Besides, Fortuno presumed on long acquaintance. It was six years since she and Robin had driven through the gates between the cypresses and looked on this house they were to make their home. When Robin had been dying Fortuno had been practical and attentive and afterwards had not minded Nan sobbing helplessly into his shoulder; he had simply soothed her like a father and given her into Maria's waiting arms with commendable tenderness.

'Mrs Baghot?' He pronounced the name charmingly. His English was always charming and much more coherent than Nan's Italian.

'Oh,' exclaimed Molly, confused, rising from the day bed. She was wearing a flowered silk kimono beneath which were visible severely practical underwear and old-fashioned stays.

'You remember Dr Fortuno,' Nan said encouragingly.

'Have we met?' Molly took his outstretched hand and smiled up girlishly into his face.

'I think the day you arrived. By the front entrance.'

'The day we arrived? Then how could I have forgotten you?'

Nan watched his striking combination of the disinter-

17

ested professional and the concerned friend. 'A natural warmth,' Aunt Dot had called it, captivated in spite of misgivings. She had come out to the villa after Robin's death 'to be of use' as she put it. For a while she and Fortuno had circled suspiciously.

'I suppose he did everything possible?'

'Everything,' said Nan.

Nan and Robin had come to the villa in '47. Though there were still ruins elsewhere the war had apparently passed by Cittavigile clinging to the flank of its remote hill. For two years after this life had been a perpetual summer holiday, even when the rain fell or the mist closed in from the mountains. After the years of looking after her mother, after the queues, worry, boredom, dread of war, Nan let herself sink into idleness as into a blessed and restoring bath after hard labour. But two years proved enough. 'I haven't anything to do,' she said to Robin. In the beginning it had been not a complaint, simply an expression of surprise. With some trepidation she had driven to the convent and offered to help with the orphans. 'Isn't that enough?' asked Robin when it seemed that her dissatisfaction grew rather than diminished. 'Of course, if the baby . . .' But the baby had not lived. Nan was not, after all, a mother with a mother's absorbing duties and preoccupations.

Then Robin's lung had collapsed and the long struggle had begun. There was no more holiday. Her time was thieved by the small stultifying routines of the sick: every minute she must keep him clean, warm, fed and entertained. A visit to the village, to the convent, became the crowning moment of the week as her world shrank to the bedroom, the bed, the wasted gasping body in it. Often she wondered where she got the strength. Even during Evelyn's last illness she had never had to be as strong as this. Sometimes she thought she only pretended such serenity, wiping his face, propping up his thinning body, making jokes for him out of trivial events – but even pretence takes strength. 'I kept going,' was her only comment to Aunt Dot afterwards.

'Dear Nan, I love you,' Robin had said with almost his last breath.

She had never doubted it. Their affection had been contained but enduring, like his for old carpets and hers – flowering secretly – for Cittavigile and the Villa Giulia. 'And there's merit in that,' Aunt Dot had written once when Nan had suggested that Robin cared as much for his old Labrador as he did for her. 'Don't underestimate his feelings.' But Aunt Dot is always full of good advice, thought Nan, and forgot it, coping with new sparks of disillusion struck by well-meaning friends. They thought Robin a substitute parent; she had married him so quickly after Evelyn died. 'Mother would never have approved,' Nan pointed out, but they had never met her and were still sceptical.

'He's years older than you,' someone said.

'Nan, darling, he fought at Ypres,' said someone else.

'Should that be held against him?' asked Nan.

At twenty-seven she had been innocent, untried. Years of bondage to Evelyn and all the new restrictions of war combined to thwart her. There were plenty of men about but if they noticed her she saw them only at a distance and vaguely, hurrying to be home every night by seven. Her mother, crippled by arthritis, could not, would not cook her own supper. Only once had Nan dared keep irregular hours, years before when her father had been alive and they had lived in Cambridge. At seventeen the demands of the flesh are irresistible. How she had burned hot and cold, desiring and dreading a glimpse of one particular face, the touch of particular hands. Evelyn, informed by well-meaning friends, said. 'I won't have my daughter meeting undergraduates. Who is he? What have you done together?'

Her father died, 'tired out by Evie', said those same friends. The house in Cambridge had to be sold. Evelyn took Nan to London. The war came. In spite of such changes Nan cried, 'Nothing much ever happens to me,' and thought Fate unkind, for other people seemed to suffer excitement and excursions and absorbing crises. She had gone to work for Stollitt and Boardman, solicitors, reluctantly. What challenges would come to her behind those heavy doors?

'Vera's left. I've been made old Stollitt's own,' she informed Evelyn lightly one evening over supper, listening for the sirens. She saw it not as promotion but as another step to complete ossification.

Forty-one was the year the shabby offices emptied of their last young men. Old Stollitt died. Young Stollitt, who was fifty, sat at his father's desk. 'I suppose we must carry on, Miss Gilman,' he said to Nan, but working in a half-empty building unnerved him and he grew anxious and difficult to please, bewailing the loss of Miss Hellyer who had rushed away to Munitions and even Miss Sampson the junior who came back to see them now and then invariably dressed in army trousers and a tight jumper.

One morning: 'Old Briston had died at last, Miss Gilman,' said Stollitt and sent her to the file for the will. As she extracted it the sirens went off. 'It's a false alarm,' the ARP warden said, meeting Nan on the stairs, the documents still in her hand. 'What about a cuppa? I just seen the old man making a run for the basement.' The kettle had just boiled when a knock heralded Robin Mortimer. 'There are planes down river,' he told them, 'and puffs of smoke.' He was one of Briston's executors, he said, and looked about for Stollitt. Stollitt remained stubbornly in the basement until the All Clear, by which time Nan and Robin and the ARP warden had drunk a whole pot of tea and reduced the secretary's office to a fug of steam and cigarette smoke.

So Miss Gilman eventually became Mrs Mortimer and the war ended and the baby died – and the big old Morris nosed in through the gates of the Villa Giulia.

'Oh, what a beautiful place,' Nan had cried.

'Signora Mortimer,' Fortuno repeated. 'Anna,' and he touched her arm.

Nan started.

'I've given Mrs Baghot a sleeping pill. She promises to take it.'

'I shall, dear. I shall be very good,' Molly assured her. She had sunk down again on the day bed and looked like some small exotic bird, head on one side.

'She seems very cheerful,' said Fortuno, leading the way downstairs.

'She has been all day. She ate an enormous dinner, everything Graziella carried up to her.'

'How sensible.'

'Or unnatural.'

His look said: You can't measure other people's grief by your own. At the front door he stopped to take her hand.

'What is there for you to worry about?' he asked.

Nan let her hand lie limp in his warm dry palm. Since Robin had died he was the only man to have touched her. Though brief and impersonal, contact with him always disturbed her. And I don't want to be disturbed, she thought. Long ago, after the baby, she had screamed when Robin tried to fold her in his arms. She had needed Aunt Dot, bracing, matter-of-fact. She had not been ready for Robin's tenderness, had not been ready to weep. 'Go away!' she had cried. 'Go away! Go away!' And such fierceness was so unlike her that Robin had been at a loss.

'Nan's never wild,' he said helplessly to Aunt Dot. He felt confused, like a small boy at a new school, not knowing names, not knowing the way.

'It's not every week she loses a baby,' replied Aunt Dot crisply.

'But I want to help.'

'Help by leaving her alone.'

'I want my baby,' howled Nan in the green and antiseptic hospital. She was being tucked up by a silent and unsympathetic nurse with legs like fence-posts.

'You'll get over it in time, Mrs Mortimer,' the consultant told her, looking briefly at his watch and thinking of his dinner.

Some things are never 'got over', Aunt Dot would have remarked, and the same thought pierced Nan where she lay curled defensively in the harsh over-laundered sheets.

'Understandably irrational,' said the consultant to the sister in the corridor. 'Only to be expected. What a pity though it was the first.'

'Other people never behave as we think they should,' Nan said to Fortuno on the steps of the Villa Giulia. 'I ought to be glad Mrs Baghot hasn't broken down in hysterics. I suppose she might have had a heart attack herself.'

'I doubt it. Her heart is very strong.'

'Do you think . . . do you think she knew he was dead when she went out into the garden?'

'Perhaps.'

Well, she's not *soprafatta dal dolore* in the least, thought Nan. Rather the opposite. She's happy. She's like . . . she's like a bird who has found the cage door open at last.

'Goodnight, Anna,' said Fortuno.

'There won't be any trouble? It was natural causes?'

'I promise you.'

She watched the red lights of the car vanish through the gates.

3

I T seemed that Major Baghot had suffered for years with a bad heart and should have had his pills with him.

'I think he lost them in Florence,' said Molly vaguely. She was a bad witness, confused and confusing. They humoured her, touched by a premonition of their own eventual senility, but she defeated rational questioning.

'There,' said Fortuno to Nan. 'I told you you didn't have to worry.'

'Poor old man,' said Maria. 'To wake in the night, no pills, no wife . . . It was all that walking, walking. She tire him out. Such a gentleman, such manners.'

'I thought he looked a bit of a bully,' retorted Nan. Really she had noticed little except that he had been fond of whisky. And should he have been drinking at all? 'Besides, Mrs Baghot must have been there when he died. She didn't realize. She didn't wake. He went quite peacefully.'

'Huh!' said Maria.

It was arranged that the Major should be buried in

the Protestant cemetery in Rome. 'So far away,' sighed Giuseppina, who imagined herself stepping on to the train with the Major's coffin and escaping Sister Angela's vigilance for ever. In the end the coffin went by road, followed only by Nan, Father Emilio – whom Nan plied with sherry, grappa and Cognac to reconcile him to heretics – and Dr Fortuno. Molly, agitated, refused to attend. Instead she walked, Maria reported, down to the village and then towards Gubbio along green hill tracks. Signor Branco had brought her back in his lorry from somewhere quite remote. But that same evening after dinner she took coffee on the terrace with the other guests and chattered indefatigably.

'What energy,' ended Maria, admiring in spite of herself.

'But only for some things,' complained Nan, for the persistent Ruddock had rung twice the day before and Molly had refused to talk to him. He had sounded frustrated but not surprised.

'I do understand, Mrs Mortimer. The truth is she's always been a little odd since . . . Oh well. She'll be quite safe with Lily.'

'Lily?'

'Her sister. You know. Spinster. Lives in Calne.'

'No, I didn't know she had a sister.'

'Well, I'm sure Miss Trewarden said she'd written. As soon as she heard, she said. Haven't any letters arrived your end?'

'Yes. Yes, I suppose . . .'

'They don't get on very well, those two.'

Nan said brightly to Molly, 'How lucky you are having a sister. I was an only child – and felt it.'

'Lily? I don't want to see her. I don't have to, do I?'

'But you don't have anybody else.'

25

'I have a son.'

'A son!'

'I used to walk him across the Parks to school. Bobs. I always called him Bobs but Edward insisted on Robert.' In an undertone she added absently, 'He liked to insist.'

'But shouldn't you . . . shouldn't he . . .'

'My dear, this Frenchwoman you have staying now. Those little dogs of hers have fleas, I'm sure of it. You really ought to speak to her.'

Nan took a straw hat and set off for the village. It was a long time since she had walked there.

'Signora, it's too hot to walk!' exclaimed Degnare when she had thankfully climbed the cold stone stairs to his office. His quick glance was critical. My old cotton frock, she thought, faded after summers of use. She had made it herself during the blitz. The word seemed strange now, like ancient slang: blitz. It seemed so long ago. Ten, eleven years? She could recall stitching close to the lamp and old Mrs Fraser from the floor above knocking to ask if they were going to the shelter.

'A glass of lemonade,' suggested Degnare and sent across to the café. He was either cheerful and loud with encouragement or, as today, anxious and inclined to treat her as an invalid.

'And how is the villa, signora?'

'I don't think Maria's very happy.'

'But you make a profit. You survive. Maria works. Does she still sing? If she sings there's no need to worry.'

'She needs more help.'

'You can't afford it.'

'I know.'

26

The lemonade came and he watched closely while she drank as if she were a child taking medicine.

'So what's all this about Mrs Baghot?'

'She says she doesn't want to leave,' said Nan.

'Well,' and he spread his hands in a these-things-are-sent-to-try-us-but-they-pass gesture. 'The funeral was only yesterday. What can you expect? She wishes to stay in the place where he died, where he breathed his last beside her.' He assumed a more tragic air. 'Where they were happy,' he added.

'I don't know if they were ever happy. But that's beside the point. What about the bills?'

'Ah, the bills. The hotel, the funeral . . . Yes, signora, of course we must be businesslike about the bills.'

'Well, what can I do?' asked Nan.

At the hairpin bends in the shade of the cypresses Nan stopped to take off a shoe and rub her aching foot. It was so long since she had climbed here like this. Once she had done so often, leaning on Robin's arm. That had been the first year or the next, she remembered, when he had been quite well. She looked out across the hills: vineyards, remote farms, green open fields, trees, distant villages. She thought: I could walk the rest of the way in bare feet – and eased her toes in the dust.

A car approached.

'Anna. *Buon giorno*,' and there was Fortuno opening a door and helping her in.

'It's so hot,' she said, 'and still only May.'

He looked under the brim of her hat. Her face was flushed and beaded with sweat, her hair stuck to her forehead.

'You need a change,' he announced abruptly after this careful examination.

'A change?'

'Of air. Of scenery. You haven't been home to England since Robin died. You haven't been back at all, have you, since you came here?'

'Home isn't England. Home is here.'

'But you are English.'

She leaned forward a little, fiddling with the brim of her hat so that he would not see the hot tears of disappointment and silly rage. 'I'd like to live here for the rest of my life. I'd like to die here. I'd like to be thought of as . . . Italian.'

'But how is that possible? You are English,' he repeated.

'Why shouldn't it be possible?'

They sat in silence for a moment. He made no move to drive on. His hand tapped the steering wheel lightly.

'You own a house in England, don't you?'

'I inherited it when my mother died. It's in a small town in Sussex. Aunt Dot lives there. She's lived there thirty years. She has tenants in the back half.'

'Why not go and see if everything's all right? After all, Aunt Dot isn't a young woman.' He put the car in gear. 'As your doctor I'd recommend a holiday.'

'And what about the villa? The season's only just beginning.'

'Close down for two weeks. Why not?'

'I can't afford to and anyway, I have bookings.'

'Close it when you haven't bookings. Don't take any more bookings. Anything. Go home.'

They turned in at the gates. Nan held grimly to the door handle. She sensed Fortuno's exasperation, the exasperation of an adult confronting a stubborn child.

'This is my home,' she told him stiffly as they drew up and the noise of the engine died away with a sigh.

'Then go to Perugia for a week to Signora Donati. She was always a good friend. She'd love to have you.'

Nan climbed out. 'How ridiculously persistent you are,' she said in a low voice and was thankful he did not hear. He leaned across to ask her to repeat it but there was a sudden screech of 'Signora! Signora!' and Maria was hurrying down the steps, her face scarlet. 'The Signora Baghot has run away to Assisi.'

'What?'

'She ordered a taxi. Goodbye, she says. All smiles and waves. I'll see the Basilica, she says. Signora, signora . . . What are we to do?'

Fortuno was laughing. 'Stop it,' said Nan. 'Do try to take things seriously. Maria, there's nothing we can do, is there?'

'But I don't think,' and Maria pressed her hands to her face, scrunching up the plump hot cheeks. 'Signora, I don't think she took any money.'

The hens had escaped their run and were gathered round the kitchen door in the courtyard under the almond tree. Antonio was summoned to catch them and there was a great squawking and flapping of wings.

'You'll put them off laying,' protested Nan. 'There'll be no eggs tomorrow.'

'It can't be helped,' said Maria.

Antonio departed with two hens in each hand. Those that were left waited until he was out of sight and then moved discreetly back to the shade, settling their feathers.

'We'll have to send down to the village for eggs,' Nan said gloomily.

'Jesus and Mary will look after us,' Maria told her.

But will Jesus and Mary look after Molly Baghot?

29

wondered Nan. She looked up to see Graziella's face at an upper window, her elegant little nose flattened by the glass. Molly and Graziella often stopped to have a conversation, one trying out sketchy English, the other eccentric Italian. 'What a lovely girl,' Molly had said.

The convent ought to turn out demure, disciplined children, eager to learn. So Nan had once thought, watching the orphans in their black smocks tripping across the village square to Mass holding hands, strictly silent. 'But you should see them in school,' Nan said to Robin after her first day as a volunteer in the nursery. Her ears still rang from the noise; her arms and thighs felt bruised from so many insistent little hands. Later, when Pia could not cope, Sister Angela sent her two of the older girls for the hotel.

'Thieves and gypsies,' cried Maria, scandalized. 'Their own parents didn't want them. Why should we?'

'But the nuns have brought them up.'

'To sew and to pray. What else can they do?' And afterwards: 'It's those girls,' Maria would say at the least evidence of imperfection. 'Ignorant ... sly ... They even look over their shoulders at Antonio.'

And: 'Don't be ridiculous,' Nan was always saying.

Now Maria, glancing up and catching sight of the smooth dark head as it withdrew, said, 'There'll be trouble with that one. Signor Arletti says the boys all hang about the convent walls for her.'

'Sister Angela will see them off. Is that the time? I need to start on the salad.'

In the kitchen garden Nan prodded her young lettuces. She was a hopeful and incompetent gardener. Evelyn had once remarked unkindly, 'It's so difficult to know exactly where Annette's talents lie.' Maybe I don't have any, Nan thought, but her fingers felt at home in the warm crumbly soil. Antonio suffered her to hoe and thin and pick the soft fruit, though often he followed her about in case she blundered, or said disparagingly, 'No, no, signora. We do it like this,' and plucked or tied up or snapped off deftly while she fumbled.

Robin had never cared for vegetables except to eat them cooked by Maria.

'Why do we pay Antonio if you're out there doing his job for him?'

'I don't do his job. I know next to nothing. I just mess about.'

'Doesn't he mind?'

'Ever so. I'm really only allowed in the piece by the fig trees.'

The young lettuces looked healthy and green. And that's all I know about them, Nan thought. The neat rows were visually satisfying: parsley, onions, tomato canes . . . She brushed her hands along the tops of the lavender hedges that divided the plots and sniffed her palms, smiling.

A whistle beyond the rose-smothered wall announced Signor Arletti with the newspapers. They came once a week and she never read them. 'They're for the guests,' she said, but by the time they arrived the guests had bought their own in Assisi or Perugia. Now as she received the bundle she saw 'Murder in Palermo' and then 'Troops in Korea. General . . .' Arletti waited. It was customary to talk for five minutes, however many of the high lonely farms he had to visit, whatever disasters might be incubating for her indoors. Today he told her that the butcher's widow had taken up with a salesman from Rome. When he said 'Rome' he spat into the fennel to show her what he thought of such a place, full of the prosperous, idle and corrupt. Then: '*Come sta la Signora Baghot?*'

'As you might expect,' Nan told him. I can hardly say she's blooming, she thought.

'What's Signora Baghot to him?' snorted Antonio who had overheard, watching the newspaper seller depart. 'He should mind his own business.'

'He wants something interesting to tell the farms up the valley. They've probably all seen her out walking.'

'Huh,' and he walked off to see if she had been interfering with the vegetables. She saw, with some satisfaction, that he had chicken feathers in his white hair.

In the house Maria hurried forward with the news. 'The police have telephoned from Assisi.'

'She's had an accident. She's been knocked down,' wailed Graziella.

'What?' demanded Nan, horrified.

'Of course not. The silly girl. She shouldn't try to listen where she's no business. Signora Baghot is with the *carabinieri*. The taxi driver made a complaint. She couldn't pay his fare.'

'Then I suppose I'll have to,' said Nan.

A darting figure, draped with flimsy scarves, flew from the drab recesses of the police station.

'Oh, how sweet of you to come,' cried Molly.

The taxi driver received his fare and an enormous tip without comment while the policeman in charge of her made constant soothing noises, clucking indulgently, patting her arm. He told her not to come out without her purse again – look at the trouble it caused – but Molly shook him off and ran away down the steps to the Morris.

32

'I'm sorry,' said Nan. More than anything she felt sorry for them, keeping Molly amused for several hours.

In the car Molly told her all about it. She did not seem able to stop talking. Her mind ranged back and forth, plucking up sensations and recollections, tossing out names, even the dishes she had hoped to have for lunch.

'And how nice that young Father Michele is,' she said as Cittavigile came in sight. 'I gave him a lift in my taxi to the next village.'

'Really?' Nan had scarcely listened to a word for the last ten miles.

'We spoke in French,' Molly informed her triumphantly.

'Does he know any?'

'Well, we mustered a few words between us. He was very kind. He said Edward was with God.'

'I hope he is.'

'But I don't believe in God.'

'You didn't tell that to Father Michele?'

'Of course not, dear. It would be so cruel. He takes it so seriously.'

Nan struggled with the gears. 'I'm sure the clutch is slipping,' she said.

'What's slipping, dear? And we talked of Graziella.'

'Graziella?'

'Such a difficult time of life, not woman, not child. All the men ogling, wanting to touch, wanting to be the first to touch.'

'You said all that in French to Father Michele?'

'No, dear. All I said to Father Michele was how beautiful she is, how charming. Goodness, I learnt my French in the eighties from an English governess.'

Here were the gates. Nan felt suddenly tired, so tired that she thought she would like to go to the meadow and lie in the grass under the cherry and sleep and sleep. It must be the drive to Assisi, she thought, the tussle with the car, the anxiety, fearing the worst. Oh, how she longed for sleep – and silence. The enervating deluge of Molly's conversation flowed on even as they came to a standstill.

'You ought to take great care of Graziella, dear.'

'The nuns take care of her.'

'But she's very fond of you. She told me so.'

'She's only my responsibility when she's here working.'

'Is she?' Molly was rearranging her scarves. 'Well, we're here. And time for a bath before dinner. How lovely.' And then, just as Nan thought: She's forgotten Graziella, she's getting out, she's going to run upstairs to her bath . . .

'Don't you remember what it was like being young?' asked Molly.

4

WHEN Nan had first come to the Villa Giulia she had felt intimidated. 'By what?' asked Robin, irritated, for surely she had only just said 'What a beautiful place,' in tones of both love and amazement. Now she wandered through the rooms neither speaking nor touching. It was a sprawling house, very old, so unlike any house she had been used to that she was at a loss.

'I wouldn't know how to live in such a place,' she said.

'You simply live in it. Why are you making problems where none exist?' demanded Robin.

The house was everything he wanted. He could sit on the terrace with a book or spend time with friends or walk to the village to drink at the café. He could drive Nan to Assisi or Spoleto and explore, like a child, her hand in his. 'We have very little money of course,' Nan wrote to Aunt Dot, but they needed very little apparently and there was no reason why this blessed contentment – 'Complacency?' wondered Aunt Dot – should ever be troubled.

'This house is seriously underfurnished,' Robin remarked several times.

'It's not. It's just right.'

They had brought only Robin's Turkish rugs from England, lozenges of colour on the cool stones, and a small writing desk that had been his mother's. The rest of the furniture was local, solid, old-fashioned. Maria thought the house looked English but Nan and Robin – particularly Robin – thought it distinctly Italian. Its only Englishness, they felt, was the mass of flowers in every room. 'There are petals everywhere,' grumbled Maria. 'Everywhere,' agreed Pia, shaking her head and making disparaging noises as she wielded dustpan and brush.

But there is no paradise on earth, Nan might have said, along with Father Emilio. She felt the first stirrings of discontent. Sometimes, before she could annihilate it, the thought came: If only I could have another child . . . Perhaps she saw the same thought in Father Emilio's eyes, but he was tactful, even tender.

'He's after your soul,' said Robin, amused.

'I hardly think so. He talks about wine,' she retorted.

Then Robin fell ill.

'It is a grave matter. I will not disguise the truth from you, signora,' said Fortuno. He was not sure how well she would take it and his English was stately and measured as if he were offering her the words to hold on to for strength.

So it was that as the weeks passed Robin's bedroom grew more 'English' and more of a contrast to the rest of the house. Medicine bottles, glasses, jugs, flowers, books, photographs . . . 'Clutter,' said Nan but it stayed, was added to: pictures, papers, bowls of fruit. It was always warm, too. 'Claustrophobic,' Nan wrote to Aunt Dot, but made a joke of it, in case it should seem disloyal. Besides, she had no authority for change. The shutters were always drawn or half-drawn so that the room was dim, even in the early morning. How she longed to throw them back, to let in the clean air, the blessed sun. But:

'I feel better in the dark,' said Robin.

'Let him have what he wants,' Fortuno warned her.

'Poor man. The dark is kind,' Maria remarked, concocting small enticing meals Robin could hardly taste.

The dark was kind, disguising a Robin wasted and reduced. He did not want Nan to see him clearly. He did not want her to know how quickly he was losing the battle. The shutters stayed closed. The room grew stuffy, crowded with the paraphernalia of illness and a great weight of false cheerfulness. How can I bear it? Nan wondered. But she bore it, smiling and calm.

Until now she had stood only in Robin's shadow. She had always lived in shadow and so never resented it. Anyway, she loved him. She relied on his advice. He encouraged and praised and guided and organized her. Like a shy puppy she had hidden behind him, looking out at the frightening world. Only later, opening the villa to strangers, did it occur to her to think: I could never have done this once. I wonder why?

A crushed flower sometimes takes a long time to rise, Dr Fortuno had told himself, thinking of her. He had always believed Robin bullied her a little, the way strong kindly men often bully inexperienced women. He noticed that in her husband's presence she never expressed opinions. Fortuno knew she had opinions because sometimes she expressed them to him in her stilted grammar-book Italian. He wondered about the baby she had lost. Stillborn, he believed. Why had there been no other? As a doctor he might ponder medical reasons but as a man he thought sadly of the endless permutations of grief and desire.

When Robin was finally, desperately ill, Nan had become another woman, cold and distant. She moved, she spoke, but in an inhuman calm, a trance. All her natural warmth was for Robin, her smiles, her supporting arms ... I'm so tired, she thought, climbing the stairs, but when she passed through the bedroom door she became the old Nan, the Nan of Stollitt and Boardman, of the register office, the London flat, the first years at the Villa Giulia, only a little thinner and more haggard, which Robin's kind darkness hid along with so much else.

Afterwards there was a natural reaction, a period of chaos. Nan was helpless and tearful. Maria could not make her eat. Degnare toiled back and forth to the villa in a valiant attempt to combine sympathy with legal duty. Letters flew to England.

'Come, there's no need for you to be ill,' Fortuno had said, finding Nan in bed at eleven in the morning, worn out with weeping. He had glimpsed her smooth pale shoulder as she turned away and the nightdress had slipped back, and the small matched knobs of her spine had looked as appealing as a child's.

'Tomorrow,' he had told her firmly, 'I want to find you in the garden, enjoying the good sun.'

But it was a week before he found her there.

'She's coming to at last,' said Aunt Dot, who had turned up about this time and put herself in charge.

'Coming to?' repeated Fortuno. 'Coming to what?'

'To herself, poor child.'

'Perhaps. But does she know who she is?'

'What a strange man,' Aunt Dot remarked to Nan,

coming to occupy the neighbouring chair on the terrace. 'I expect it's just his English really.'

'I couldn't have asked for a better doctor.'

'Well, I'm glad to hear it. He has beautiful manners, of course. Good-looking too.'

'All his women patients fall in love with him.'

'How silly of them.'

'I'm teasing, Aunt Dot.'

'Isn't he married?'

'Years ago he was. She died. Would being married make him safe?'

'Safer maybe.'

Nan smiled. It was a relief to smile after so much weeping. The sun was warm on her bare legs.

'Yes, she's coming to,' said Aunt Dot.

But: 'She's not the same,' confided Maria to Antonio. To whatever self she had come it was not the old self. When she smiled now it was not her old shy sweet smile, it was vague and distracted. She forgot things. And yet . . . and yet she seemed capable of calculating determination. In six months or a little more the villa was a hotel.

'She always had backbone,' reported Aunt Dot to the elderly tenant in the back regions of the house in Sussex. 'She put up with Evelyn after all, didn't she?' Three letters in quick succession arrived from this tenacious and yet queerly distraught Nan and in bed, having put them away, Aunt Dot was sleepless and anxious. Is she going to be happy? she asked herself.

Father Emilio was never anxious. He had seen so much grief, and the war had made so many widows.

'You've been very brave,' he told Nan. 'Things aren't so bad now, are they?'

They were drinking wine on the terrace. 'No,' replied Nan. 'Things aren't so bad.'

'Of course it's difficult,' he continued. 'But difficulties pass. God sends us in new directions.'

Nan's hair was twisted in a loose bundle at the nape of her neck. In the dappled shade it gleamed here and there a dull gold. He thought God might easily send her in the direction of another marriage but it would, naturally, be imprudent to say so. He sat admiring her, turning over his stock of well-worn phrases to find the most suitable.

She said abruptly, 'Dr Fortuno says I'll always be a stranger here. Is that true?'

'A stranger?'

'An Englishwoman among Italians.'

'But you are an Englishwoman among Italians.'

'And is that all I'll ever be?'

'Ah,' said Father Emilio softly. He rubbed the side of his beaky nose. 'Here in Umbria a man from the next village is a foreigner.'

'Then there's no hope at all,' sighed Nan and smiled so ruefully that he put out a hand and clasped it over hers.

'For you, signora,' he said consolingly, 'anything is possible.'

'Maria,' said Nan. 'Is anything the matter with Graziella?'

'Perhaps love,' replied Maria. She was stirring the *sugo* in the great pan. Steam from the boiling pasta wreathed between them.

'Love?'

'*Si.* Love. Who knows?'

Graziella had been crying in the garden. Nan had seen her from the terrace. When she went down and between

40

the little formal hedges to see what was going on she had been confronted by a pale desperate face, touchingly wet, tears still caught in the lower lashes. 'Graziella cries like an angel,' Giuseppina had once said. Giuseppina only grew blotched and puffy with grief like other human beings.

'What's wrong?' Nan asked.

'Nothing. Nothing,' and the girl had fled back to the house.

So: 'Is anything the matter with Graziella?' Nan demanded of Maria, and Maria thought love was the matter. That's absurd, thought Nan. She's only sixteen. But was it absurd? Sixteen was surely as good an age for love as any. At sixteen I was still a child, remembered Nan, no awareness of men, no breasts even.

Over the account books she thought of Aunt Dot in Sussex with whom, angular and retarded, she had spent a liberated holiday; liberated from Evelyn at least, and from strict bedtimes and over-anxiety about whether she wore a coat or had changed her vest. Aunt Dot scorned vests. She had a dozen portraits of herself in the nude, all by different artists. 'But I was young then,' she would say. 'Like you.' Since the war, she said, she had grown decrepit. 'But so has England,' she wrote. There had been such problems with food, with fuel, though the sense of endless struggle was receding. Nan though of rain on green Sussex lanes and of the great lift of the Downs.

I don't know where I belong, she thought.

Then: Molly Baghot isn't going to pay her bills, is she?

Graziella can't be in love.

Dr Fortuno thinks I'm a weak silly vacillating woman.

Father Emilio hopes to convert me to Rome.

Maria says she has piles.

She threw down her pen and snatched up a cardigan from the chair, hurrying out across the hall and through the front door. Before she closed it behind her she heard the chink of coffee cups from the terrace, Molly's high excited voice, laughter, an exclamation. She half-ran up the drive, feeling the dust getting in her shoes, feeing the cool air against her face. By the time she reached the gates frustration and whatever else had been blown away. She leaned her head against the stone pillar, empty and at peace.

'Signora! Signora! Quick! Quick!'

'Maria? Now what?'

For there was Maria struggling towards her, gasping, both hands clutched to her breast.

'Come. Come quickly.'

'What is it?' Another Major Baghot? wondered Nan, trembling. 'Maria, *che ha successo?*'

They hurried round the villa through the garden, past the sentinel figs, the urns full of rosemary. There was still the low uninterrupted murmur of conversation from the terrace. 'Hush,' said Maria, keeping to shadow, leading the way to the meadow.

'*Ecco la,*' she said at last.

Antonio stood by the cherry tree. At his feet lay a body.

'It's Don Michele,' said Nan, stooping. She could see very little.

She sensed they were waiting for her to take command. Were there murderers, she thought wildly, murderers in her own garden? But what had he been doing here? She bent over him again. His hair was soft and unruly under her exploring fingers, then sticky and matted. Anxiously she put her other hand on the harsh black of his cassock and felt the young heart thumping strongly.

'*Non è morto*,' she reported, flooded with relief.

'That's a blessing then,' remarked Antonio.

Between them they carried him circumspectly to the house. The terrace was dark by now but like thieves they crept through greenery to the kitchen courtyard. Then they laid him on the great old table in front of Maria's stove.

'We need Dr Fortuno,' said Nan. The head wound was messy and she worried that he did not wake. Antonio chafing him with rough hands, Maria wafting burnt feathers, even brandy failed to rouse him.

'*Pronto*,' came Fortuno's voice. Nan saw that her fingers, holding the receiver, were smeared with blood.

'Will you come?' she asked.

'Of course I shall come.'

By the time he did, the kitchen looked like a battle-field. 'Well, heads always bleed and bleed,' Nan said to Maria. The smell of burning, strong drink and garlic hung in the air. Father Michele reclined on the table with his head on a cushion like an effigy.

'The wound needs stitching. No sign of a depressed fracture. He's young and tough. Maria, another lamp,' said Fortuno, bracingly efficient.

In an undertone to Nan he asked, 'What was he doing in your garden?'

'I've no idea,' said Nan.

When he woke Father Michele was temporarily in-coherent. Nan wondered, with sudden insight, if guilt and not concussion was the cause. He denied that any-one had attacked him. He said he had run away from a great dog, a savage brute lurking on the road. He had scrambled over the crumbling stone wall at the foot of the meadow and fallen.

'Then I don't remember anything,' he said.

'I see,' said Nan, who saw only that this was rather too fanciful to explain such extensive injuries.

'I'll take him back to the village,' Fortuno told her.

'He'll face an inquisition by Don Emilio.'

'Not tonight. I shall forbid it.'

Nan looked down at the young square face, already relaxed again in sleep. 'He tries so hard,' she said.

'At what?'

'Being a priest. It's so important to him but it seems so difficult. It doesn't make him very happy.'

'Perhaps he tries too hard,' suggested Fortuno sourly. 'It's sometimes the sign of conscience. He may doubt his vocation.'

He knows what's going on, Nan thought, looking into his darkly amused face. Does Maria know? But what *is* going on? Conspirators, they arranged Father Michele in the doctor's car, stepping back in guilty shock when the engine roared into the stillness.

'Well,' said Maria as they went back to the kitchen and looked around at the mess. 'He'll have some explaining to do.'

'He doesn't remember anything,' said Nan, putting the cork back in the brandy.

'Nor will he, if he's wise,' and Maria shuffled off to fetch a cloth.

The next morning Father Emilio toiled up between the cypresses and Nan found it was she who was to undergo the inquisition.

'Why was he in your garden, signora?'

'I really don't know. But he wasn't in the garden. He was walking up the road and a dog ran at him, he said, so he jumped over the wall into my meadow and fell and knocked himself out.'

'What dog?'

'I don't know.'

'There are no dogs.'

'There are shepherds' dogs. They can be savage.'

'But where was the shepherd?'

Nan drew an indignant breath. 'Are you suggesting Don Michele is lying? Or that I am?'

'No, no,' and he was contrite at once, taking her hand in an avuncular reassuring clasp. 'Nothing of the kind. But he had retired early to bed. He had said goodnight to me. Why was he walking in the road by your property so late in the night? You are only a little way from the village.'

'Have you asked Don Michele all this?'

'No. No. He's not well. And Fortuno warned me against it.'

'I expect he couldn't sleep and went out for a walk.'

'But he did not use the door.'

'How can you be sure?' Nan demanded.

Father Emilio was looking at her dubiously. He is trying to catch me out, she thought, astonished. But I don't know anything. I don't know as much as he does. How can I be caught in a falsehood?

'I'll ask Maria to bring you a glass of wine,' she said briskly. 'I'm sorry. I'm so very busy this morning,' and she left him standing quite forlorn, his hat in his hand, gazing after her through the vine leaves.

5

'SO the young man was waiting by the cherry tree in the moonlight,' said Molly, who always came to know everything. 'For whom, I wonder?'

'What young man?'

'The dear little priest with the wayward hair. So very young. He could be my grandson.'

'How did you hear about it?'

'Father Emilio asked me if I'd ever met any dogs on the road. Of course I asked why.'

Anyone else, Nan thought, might simply have answered yes or no.

'There wasn't a moon,' she pointed out, irritated.

'I don't suppose it mattered. Except with a moon he would have seen who did it.'

'Who did what?' Life had been tranquil before Molly Baghot had arrived, Nan thought, and she wished it would be so again.

'Well, hit him. Poor boy. Someone must have hit him.' Molly's piquant little monkey face smiled up at her. 'It must have been a rival, don't you think?'

'I think Mrs Baghot is quite mad,' Nan told Maria.

'Isn't that what I always said?' and then seriously, confidentially: 'She's not safe to be out.'

The telegram was addressed to Nan and came up with the newspapers. 'More killings in Palermo' she noticed as she received the bundle between suddenly nerveless hands. Was it Aunt Dot? Was she ill? Dead?

'Please arrange Marion Baghot travel Calais soon as possible. Notify train and date. Ruddock.'

'They want me back,' said Molly. 'It's the will, you see.'

'The Major's will?'

'He told me. He's left his money to Lily so that she can look after me. I have to live in Wiltshire. You can't imagine . . . Sofas with doghairs, vicars to tea, Boots Library.'

'Perhaps if you spoke to Mr Ruddock . . .'

'I don't want to speak to him. I don't want to live with Lily. I don't want to go back.'

'What am I do with her?' Nan asked Degnare. She was sitting in his office and her head throbbed; she felt a little strange. I'm going to be ill, she thought quite happily. She was never ill. She thought how pleasant it would be to renounce responsibility and lie back in a chair on the terrace and drink wine, looking up through the vine leaves.

'What am I to do?' she repeated.

'I shall speak to this Ruddock.'

Nan sighed. She felt crushed, overwhelmed. She had put on a suit for this visit, determined to look a little elegant. Italian women were elegant – and bold, self-possessed. He thinks I'm ridiculous, an English mouse, she thought.

'I'll leave it all to you,' she said.

*

The house was quiet when she returned. More roses had dropped their petals on the hall table and she swept them up automatically, walking through to the terrace to scatter them over the wall. It was almost dinner-time. She could hear subdued voices from behind the half-drawn shutters above where her guests were changing. There was a permeating fragrance of lamb and basil.

Nan sat on the wall and brushed the last petal over into the lavender and rosemary below. From here she could see the overgrown gravel path between the uncut hedges, the stone seat, the high wall with its roses.

'*Buona sera*,' said Fortuno. He was sitting smoking by the steps.

'Is anyone ill?' she asked, half-serious.

'I hope not. I wanted to see you about Graziella. Sister Angela was hoping . . .'

Nan brushed at the skirt of the dark suit where it was smudged from sitting on the wall. 'Can't Sister Angela come and talk to me herself?'

'She is trying to be discreet.'

'Discreet?'

'People might talk. There's enough talk already.'

'I haven't heard any,' Nan announced. 'What are people talking about?'

He drew on the cigarette and looked away down the garden. She felt he was amused.

'Sister Angela thinks Graziella should go to Perugia. The convent there will find her a job.'

'Why? What's wrong with her job here?'

'Nothing. Nothing at all. But Sister Angela is . . . concerned.'

Nan moved a little closer, breathing in the acrid smoke of his cigarette. 'I don't understand.'

He stood up. 'I can hear your guests,' he said. Somewhere in the house was movement and low voices. 'I told Sister Angela you knew nothing.'

'I would like to know,' and as he still listened, his head tilted, she added: 'Forget my guests. They hardly ever come on the terrace before dinner.'

'Have you thought Graziella might be in love?'

'Is she? So the boy is unsuitable.'

'She's very young.'

'But still . . . To hurry her away to Perugia means the nuns are worried. Who is he?'

Fortuno stubbed out his cigarette on the wall. 'But you found him in your own garden. You bathed his wound and defended him to Don Emilio like a little cat. I've heard all about it.'

There was a silence during which Nan realized that she was, inevitably, the last to know. 'My darling, you're so innocent,' Robin had said once, amazed and gratified and touched all at the same time. Indeed, it had been her innocence which had attracted him in the first place. She was neither shy nor ignorant but attacked life with a puzzled and desperate ingenuity. It was easy, perhaps, to make her dependent on him.

'I suppose I'm just a fool,' she said resignedly to Fortuno. But how was it everyone else knew – if they really knew – and I didn't? she wondered. What did I miss? What was there to see?

'I'm surprised you had no suspicions,' he said.

'But I hardly ever see Don Michele. Only in the village.'

'Don Emilio has had suspicions for months, but he has only circumstantial evidence and no hard facts. If Graziella could be . . .'

'Spirited away? Oh, I see. It's all Graziella's fault.'

'She's very beautiful,' began Fortuno.

'And Don Michele's very young. But is one to be a crime and the other a pardonable condition? I'd say Graziella was too beautiful to be at the mercy of incontinent boys and Don Michele too much of an incontinent boy to be a priest.'

Fortuno's expression grew wary. So there's a tigress behind the bush, he thought, amused. 'Don't you think they're better parted before the mischief's done?'

'Perhaps it's done already.'

Her face was alive. He had never seen so many emotions chase each other before, each one deepening the colour in her skin: rage, disappointment, pity, rage again. She stood very straight, her head thrown up. The dark suit, which he had never seen her wear, gave her presence. Was she going to fight, then, to keep Graziella at the Villa Giulia? Did he need to point out that it was a serious matter, a very serious matter, for a priest to be found copulating under a cherry tree? He tried to, quite amiably, but Nan was having none of it. 'Isn't the cherry tree rather an irrelevance?' was all she said. At this he laughed and to his relief she smiled, though it was a grudging, a restricted smile. The next moment she looked at her watch and exclaimed that it was dinner-time, she should have changed, she could hear Molly Baghot on the stairs, she must run. But she paused long enough to say, 'I think I'm surprised at you,' adding in a low and almost bitter tone: 'Running Sister Angela's errands. Couldn't she come herself?' It was with astonishing satisfaction that she saw the faint flush under his brown skin. A small hit for Graziella, she thought.

'I'm sure Sister Angela wants to speak to you herself.'

'Don't worry. I want to speak to her.'

Molly, on the bottom stair, caught the full force of Nan's blazing eye.

'Have you quarrelled, dear? Is that Dr Fortuno?'

'On the terrace? There's no one on the terrace. Do go in to dinner, Mrs Baghot.'

'Molly.'

'Molly. Maria will be upset if you're late.'

'I suppose she will. Are you sure there's nobody on the terrace?'

'Nobody.'

Aunt Dot wrote to say that the tenant in the back half of Laburnum Lodge had died. 'And in such nice weather,' she added as if it might, with more effort, have been avoided. Nan, reading the letter twice with a perceptible sinking of the heart, wondered if Aunt Dot was trying to communicate something of greater importance.

'It's a burden for an old lady,' said Degnare when she told him. 'A gentle, retired old lady. To advertise, to show people round, to make sure of the rent . . . You ought to have an English agent, a man of business.'

'An agent would cost money. Besides . . .' Besides, Aunt Dot was steel. Or was she? What about those suspicions of things unsaid? 'Aunt Dot likes to feel useful,' she ended lamely.

'Still, signora, an old lady . . .'

'She wouldn't like to hear you say that. Not in that tone.'

'Then the legal aspects . . .'

'Aunt Dot always had a good nose for trouble.'

'And fixing the rent. How are rents in England?'

'She likes the challenge.'

If she kept cutting him off in mid-sentence he would

eventually raise his hands in desperation and change the subject. Nan knew this. And since he had no material interest in the house in Sussex or in Aunt Dot this would happen sooner rather than later. She had only mentioned it at all to fill an awkward pause in their inevitable skirmishings about Molly Baghot.

'We have achieved nothing, signora,' he suddenly announced in a mournful and ponderous voice. 'Look. Look,' and he pushed across his neat total of Molly's debts, great and small. Nan, irresistibly reminded of her maths teacher attempting the hopeless task of reconciling her to sine and cosine, leaned forward obediently.

'It's really all this?'

'All that. Are your figures different?'

'But you said you'd spoken to Ruddock.'

'Indeed. And *he* only repeats that we must claim against the Major's estate in due course.'

'Can't he advance something? How does he expect Mrs Baghot to manage? She ran out of cash days ago.'

'He is adamant,' declared Degnare, and then added, for effect: '*Ostinato, inflessibile.*'

'Perhaps we should be more adamant ourselves,' said Nan.

There followed half an hour of explanations, profound and prolonged explanations. Lawyers take a long time to come to the point, thought Nan, and mentally yawned.

'All we can do is what they ask,' Degnare concluded. 'Put her on the train. Wash your hands of her.'

'Only I'll have to pay for the ticket, and her meals, and something extra in case she's held up or gets stranded in Calais. I thought you were demanding I stop supporting her, not . . .'

'This way you get rid of her. Otherwise . . .'

Nan, who in groping in her bag for a handkerchief in which to sneeze away the effects of Degnare's hair oil, had accidentally pulled out Aunt Dot's letter, thought that the smell of English privet and wallflowers and aubretia rose from the envelope.

'Otherwise I may have her with me for life. Yes, I see.'

'Signora, you have been kind and generous. You've done so much, so much. But there are limits . . . There must be limits.'

'I suppose so.'

'No. No. There must be.'

'Perhaps,' said Nan.

'Men seldom listen to women,' she said to Maria whom she found shelling eggs in the kitchen.

'No?' and Maria stared with small suspicious eyes, judging this new mood. 'But why do the English like boiled eggs with their picnics?'

'I mean they don't listen in order to take them seriously,' continued Nan. 'They listen the way grown-ups listen to children. At the appropriate moment they say "Yes, well done", or "Very nice, dear", and turn away to more important things.'

Maria swept up the eggshells, considering. 'Perhaps this only happens in England,' she suggested.

'This happens in Cittavigile,' snapped Nan.

'Oh, Signor Degnare . . .' Maria shuffled into the first of the big larders and her voice came from between the hanging salamis, the great hams. 'He's a lawyer. Lawyers are paid to talk and talk and look pompous.'

'Well, I feel worn out. He went on and on. Is this food for the Prescotts? It doesn't seem enough.'

'No, no. This is for Signora Baghot.'

'Molly Baghot? Why? Where's she going?' Ever since the escapade in Assisi they had tried to limit her wanderings to the hill and the village.

'I don't know. But she was so cheerful when she ordered it. Her eyes sparkled. Signora,' and Maria leaned heavily on the table where the naked eggs and the new bread and the glistening prosciutto all waited. 'Signora, she's a little mad.'

'I know,' said Nan.

At midday Nan was down in the meadow picking up the stones that had fallen from the boundary wall and lodging them back precariously, scratching her hands. She knew it was absurd to be out in the heat. It was difficult to stoop and still keep her straw hat on. Only she had wanted to be alone and out of the house. More and more these last few days she had felt she needed to escape from the house. She needed to think about Graziella, Father Michele – why had he been in her meadow so late at night? – Molly Baghot, Aunt Dot.

After twenty minutes she stood up, easing her back. Sweat trickled into her eyes. The number of stones about her in the grass seemed the same as when she had begun.

Tonight I must speak to Graziella, she thought. Then I must tackle Molly about trains. And I must write to Aunt Dot. Is she too old and tired to carry on? It's not really a big house ... It *is* a big house and she is old.

A movement on the road caught her eye. A bicycle wobbled into view.

'Signora, *buon giorno*. But you should be indoors,' declared Father Emilio, looking over the wall.

'I think I should,' agreed Nan.

'I've just seen Mrs Baghot in an olive grove on the road by Concini's. She too looked hot.'

Nan took off her hat and fanned herself. 'Was she eating her picnic?'

'Picnic? No, signora. She was reading a book.'

'I expect she'd already eaten.'

'Who knows?' Father Emilio stroked his chin. 'But she was happy. She smiled as she read.'

6

THE Prescotts had a small child, a boy, who ran in and out making train noises and aeroplane noises and leaving dusty footprints on the tiles. The Italians smiled indulgently. 'How beautiful he is,' sighed Giuseppina. 'He is an angel,' said Maria, and at every opportunity put out a hand to stroke his close gold curls.

'Why don't they keep that child quiet?' demanded Mrs Holland, who moved from terrace to sitting-room to terrace to avoid him.

'Modern parents,' said Miss Elwes. 'No idea of discipline.'

Nan too was sure the Prescotts never thought of discipline. 'If they think at all it's only of themselves,' she said to Maria. They seemed armoured with indifference. The child played alone and untended. Nobody ever looked to see if he had fallen down the terrace steps or was swinging dangerously on the vine.

'Signora Prescott is pretty,' said Graziella, carrying in plates for dinner. 'She wears nice clothes.'

'Everything so beautifully made. He spends all his money on her. You can tell. But look at you!' and Maria jabbed a spoon accusingly. 'Is that a clean dress? Is that a clean apron?'

Graziella, whose eyelids were no longer pink, Nan noticed, stuck out her tongue.

'Graziella, come and see me after dinner, please. As soon as you've served coffee.' She was still a child, Nan thought, and worried about how she might sensibly conduct this evening's little talk.

Maria was silent. Graziella looked startled and then rebellious. She thought she was to be reprimanded for being cheeky. She said, '*Si*, signora,' and the long fine eyelids came down to hide her contempt.

Nan hurried to the dining-room to check the tables knowing that nothing would be out of place. The Prescotts were on the terrace outside, the man talking, the woman silent. Was he reading from a guidebook? The low voice droned on and on.

She was still so young, Nan thought, the pretty Mrs Prescott. She must have had the child at twenty or twenty-one and still kept the freshness of extreme youth. It was spoilt a little by her sulkiness. Was she affected by the heat, or boredom, or the constraints of never being properly alone? Her blue eyes were undeniably tragic, and a true blue, unlike Nan's which were so changeable. 'How seldom she smiles,' Nan said to Maria.

The spoons and forks were exactly aligned. Five minutes to the gong, Nan thought, smoothing the perfect cloths.

'Oh,' exclaimed Molly Baghot, tripping in, 'are the Prescotts outside? Such dear people. But he really doesn't know what to do with such a baby now he's got her.'

'It's a little boy,' corrected Nan.

'I meant his wife. There must be twenty-five years between them. Miss Elwes says he's been married before but she died, poor thing, and the grown-up children all scandalized he's chosen someone young enough to be their sister. Such a shame. He's not a very sensitive man either, is he? Built for action not thought. The modern world has nothing for him, nothing at all, only years of respectable toing and froing between his office and his lovely house and his club and bridge and golf and cocktails. Don't you feel sorry for him?'

'I hadn't thought about it,' Nan said truthfully. 'Molly, about getting the train to England.'

'My dear, can't I stay a little longer?'

'I'm fully booked at the end of this week. I shall need your room.' Nan hated to sound hard. She seemed to hear her own words from a distance as if they fell independently and were harder than the little round pebbles on the road to Cittavigile.

'Of course. Of course I'll go, dear. Until Friday then.' A whiff of lavender water rose from the chiffon scarf flung round the neck of the plain grey dress which was Molly's concession to changing for dinner. 'You mustn't look so serious. You're quite right. I should go. I should.'

Nan felt wrung with guilt. She put a hand on Molly's thin and brittle arm. 'If . . .' she began.

'I ring the gong,' announced Maria, appearing in the doorway. '*Va bene?*'

Nan removed her hand. '*Va bene*,' she said.

'Perugia! Perugia!' cried Graziella, alight with indignation.

Sister Angela had not spoken. It's been left to me, thought Nan, and grew as indignant as the girl.

'Didn't you know what would happen? He *is* a priest.'

'I didn't ask to love him.'

'I suppose not,' and Nan stared down at her own hands in her lap, held lightly together and ringless except for the narrow gold band 'which means nothing now' she thought. She moved it up and down against the knuckle. She had never dreamed of taking it off until this moment.

'Signora,' whispered Graziella, coming to kneel on the floor by Nan's chair. 'You have loved. You know what it's like.'

Looking into the young face, into the glowing dark eyes, Nan thought: But I don't. Not really. I never burned like this. Only a very little and all to no purpose. Mother saw to that. She heard her own voice say calmly, 'I'll speak to Sister Angela. But . . . you know as well as I do, there's nothing I can . . .'

Graziella dropped her head on Nan's knee as if, by such a gesture, she conferred responsibility for her happiness. Nan put a hand reluctantly on the smooth and silky hair.

'I'll do my best. But you know there isn't any future for you both. Unless . . . unless he stops being a priest.'

Graziella said, her voice muffled in Nan's lap, 'God gave us to each other. It can't be wrong. God will help us.'

'I hope so,' said Nan fervently. She had always been a little frightened of Sister Angela. Another unpleasant talk, she thought. And I haven't written to Aunt Dot yet. I could make her laugh telling her about all this: forbidden passion under the cherry tree, Father Michele wounded, Graziella banished . . .

'Graziella, what was Don Michele doing in my meadow so late at night?'

'He thought I was here, staying the night.' Sometimes, if Nan gave a small party for one of the guests, a birthday, an anniversary, the girls went to bed at the villa. 'He had a message to meet me.'

'Then who sent the message?'

But Graziella shook her head. 'Who can say?' Her eyes were full of tears. 'They're all against us. All of them. Only you are kind, you and the Signora Baggotta. You are the only kind people in the world.'

The Prescott child fell ill.

'Bah, it's nothing,' said Maria who had brought up eight children.

'We must have a doctor, Mrs Mortimer,' said Prescott, hurrying to Nan.

'Call Dr Fortuno,' Nan instructed Giuseppina.

The morning was misty. 'Is it going to rain?' asked Mrs Holland who did not expect rain to fall while she was on holiday. Mrs Prescott did not come down to breakfast. 'I hope it's nothing serious,' said Molly when Fortuno's noisy car pulled up and the doctor was seen to tread his familiar path up the wide stairs and along the corridor to the bedroom where the Major had died, where Robin had died. Mrs Prescott had insisted the child go in the big double bed. 'Which means I have to sleep in Dickie's cot, I suppose?' remarked Prescott with rather forced heartiness.

'It isn't a cot, Alan, it's a proper single bed,' said his wife. 'Don't be silly.'

'Well, what's wrong?' asked Nan when Fortuno came down.

'I don't know.'

'But you must know. You're a doctor.'

He put his bag on the hall table by the bowl of

flowers. He reached to touch a petal. 'She's very beautiful,' he said.

For a moment she thought he might be talking about
flowers.

'Mrs Prescott? Is she? But what about the little boy?'

'Too much sun. Too much strange food. Too much
excitement.'

'Is that all?'

'What more do you want? He's not going to die like
the old Major, if that's what you're worried about.'

She had wounded his feelings the other day. Was this
some sort of childish revenge? She said crossly, 'I
thought it might be measles.' For some reason measles
sounded so English. She had had measles at school and
had been shut up for weeks, the curtains drawn, the
doctor in and out, in and out, four other girls crammed
in the iron cots either side, and only two letters from
home, Evelyn sounding accusing and resentful.

'Measles!' He laughed at the very idea. 'No, no. He
has a slight temperature and a slight stomach ache. He's
enjoying both because they guarantee him his mother's
attention.'

'That's what he needs,' retorted Nan. 'They leave
him to himself. He's only four.'

'Well, he'll be in bed all day. I'll call again later.'

'Call again?'

'So the child is still ill?' said Father Emilio, sampling
French wine on the terrace the next day. 'It isn't catching, is it?'

'Dr Fortuno says not.'

'This is good,' taking another mouthful. 'I won't say
anything against French wine.' He spoke as if he could
say a great deal against the French themselves. 'You're

61

a chauvinist,' she had told him once and he had agreed vehemently: 'Yes, yes. Naples is the only place on earth for me. Everywhere else is . . .' and he had flicked his fingers. 'I don't even know why I bother with this country hole, all these mountain peasants who speak like this,' and he gave a demonstration, holding his nose.

'The French would be overwhelmed to know you approve,' Nan said. She refilled his glass. It was obvious that her sarcasm was lost on him. She was aware that so much was always being lost between her English thoughts and her Italian expressions.

'The French, huh!' and he raised his wine and looked at its colour as if, after all, he hoped to find fault.

'How is Don Michele?'

'Better. He'll take early Mass tomorrow.'

'And the dog?'

'The dog?' He looked slyly at her. Wondering what I know? thought Nan. 'The dog is in hiding. He hasn't been seen again.'

They looked at each other. He was a difficult man. Robin had once said he was pickled in his faith and its prejudices. Thin and austere, he meant business. Poor Father Michele, thought Nan. But she remembered how, when Robin had been ill, Father Emilio had been consoling and in his own way unfailingly kind. During those months he had set aside their differences. She had come to look on him as a friend and since then had treated him to these wine tastings, learning from him: 'for I know nothing about wine,' she had confessed.

'Your husband. Now, *he* knew.'

'Yes. But the cellar's mine now. I have to know what's in it. I have to restock it.'

The French wine was pale and dry.

'Is that Graziella I hear singing?' Father Emilio asked.

'No. Maria.'

The name 'Graziella' seemed to hang in the air. Nan felt suddenly compelled to ask, 'What do they do to priests who misbehave?'

'Misbehave?'

'Oh, I don't know. Neglect their duties, dabble in black magic, run away with married women.'

'Married women?' cried Father Emilio.

There was the distant slamming of a car door, the sound of mechanical distress. 'Dr Fortuno needs some new transport,' remarked Nan.

'What married women?' persisted Father Emilio.

'The doctor has called three times.'

'That means the child is really ill.'

'His mother is young and lovely.'

'Ah,' said Father Emilio.

'The doctor's adorable,' Claire Prescott told Nan. It was very late and Nan, seeing the light under the door and finding both mother and child awake, had fetched hot milk from the kitchen. By the time she returned with it the boy was asleep, curled up, breathing easily.

'How kind of you. I'll drink it,' Claire said. 'It's silly to waste it.'

'I was a little worried when I saw the doctor back again,' Nan told her.

'The doctor's adorable. He pays attention. He really seems concerned. I believe he makes Dickie feel better just by walking in and saying hello.'

All the months Robin had been ill Nan had dreaded Fortuno's arrival. She had grown weary of his constant attendance, always bracing, always sustaining. I want to be left alone, the voice had cried inside her. Why can't I be weak and hysterical if I want, in private, shut away? Robin would never know. I can't go on and on and on being calm and strong. I can't. She had grown to hate Fortuno's step on the stair.

'Well, if there's anything else, just ring. Maria goes to bed at twelve but in an emergency . . .'

There was no emergency here and not even the fondest mother could invent one. The child slept with a faint smile, his rounded cheeks a normal pink, one hand tucked beneath his chin.

'I'm sure we'll be all right.' The girl smiled too and all the petulance left her face and left it young and 'pure' said Nan to herself. No wonder Prescott had taken her in the teeth of family hostility. No wonder Fortuno hurried cheerfully and unnecessarily to her son's bedside. 'We'll manage until the doctor comes again in the morning.'

He came twice the following day and Nan found the growl of his car engine punctuating her routine. The child was sitting up and growing bored but Claire Prescott had turned the big bedroom into a fortress whose walls were to be breached only by her hero.

'He has a hero's face,' Nan told Maria.

'He has a satyr's face. A *satiro*,' replied Maria.

Nan was in the kitchen studying the new picnic list. 'They could eat well and cheaply in Assisi. Or Spoleto. Or anywhere at all,' she said.

'Signora Holland says she's tired of paintings and churches and old stones. She likes to walk among the flowers and look at the mountains, the trees, the vines.'

'While eating a boiled egg, no doubt.'

'The Signora Holland doesn't like eggs,' stated Maria.

It's no good, thought Nan, I shall never achieve sarcasm in a foreign language.

'The Signora Holland is a good woman,' continued Maria unexpectedly.

Mrs Holland was overbearing and astringent, Nan thought, and probably dominated her village committees, her vicar, the local Women's Institute and certainly everybody in an inferior social position. What, then, did Maria mean by 'a good woman'?

'You're tired, signora,' Maria said, patting Nan's arm. 'You need a rest. Don Emilio has exhausted you talking so much about wine and the catechism.'

'I don't think we mentioned the catechism. Do you really think he hopes to convert me?'

'Of course.'

'Poor man. He ought to concentrate on the souls he has and give mine up as a bad job.'

The picnic list fluttered across the table as Maria sailed past on her way to the larders. Nan put out a hand to immobilize it and, glancing down, re-read the names.

'Why have you underlined Mrs Baghot?' she asked.

'Underlined? Oh, yes, yes. She wants two picnics. She says walking makes her so hungry.'

Early that morning Nan had written to Aunt Dot. 'I've put off starting this letter several times,' she began. She had always been honest with Aunt Dot. After two or three lines she put down her pen and rubbed her fingers as if they and not her brain were making writing difficult. 'Don't do anything about another tenant yet. I think I need time to decide what's best . . .' The words trailed away. Somewhere a car door banging indicated the arrival of the two girls, brought from the convent by Antonio. Another day was beginning.

I'll finish it later, she thought thankfully, and thrust everything to the back of the desk and closed it.

'You should never put things off,' Evelyn had said to the long-ago Nan.

'I forgot.'

'That's even worse. Invitations should be answered at once. Whatever will they think?'

'But Mother, I don't really want to go. What can I say?'

'Of course you must go.'

I shall disgrace you, Nan thought bitterly. I shall do all the wrong things.

Perhaps it was her misfortune that she never did.

'They're like children,' said Maria.

'Even Mrs Holland?'

'Even Mrs Baghot. Like children they want to run on the grass and eat with the fingers.'

'Mrs Baghot is going back to England at the end of the week.'

'I know. *Poverina*. She has to go back to this cruel sister and the fog and no food. It's still like the wartime in England, she says: grey, sad, no food.'

'Not according to Aunt Dot. Perhaps Mrs Baghot wants you to feel sorry for her.'

'I do feel sorry for her.'

But not, thought Nan, for Graziella in love with a priest. This seemed to have put the girl outside the range of Maria's normally extensive sympathy.

A stray word surfaced belatedly. '*Cruel* sister?' Nan asked, taken aback.

'I could tell you things . . .' began Maria, coming to a stand with her hands full of eggs and a rapt expression on her face.

'I don't want to know,' said Nan firmly.

Another difficult day, she thought. Her emotions were under siege. Making her appointment with Sister Angela she had had to be deliberately evasive. 'She can't make me discuss it over the phone,' she said to Maria, but Maria had simply tossed up her head and said something Nan could not catch. 'What is it about?' asked Sister Angela sweetly. 'I'd rather not say,' Nan told her, surprising herself by her own briskness, the pleasant but businesslike way she had agreed a time, had said '*A piu tardi*,' as if she were looking forward to it.

The Morris defeated her by refusing to start.

'*Putana*,' remarked Antonio, called to help. 'She's old and overworked, signora. She's tired.'

'You never seem to have as much trouble,' said Nan crossly.

'May I help?' Alan Prescott strolled into the kitchen courtyard and stood by the garage door with his hands in his pockets. He looked dispirited and discontented.

'I'm afraid not. Even if we all pushed it wouldn't do any good.'

'Then may I give you a lift somewhere?'

'I have to go to the convent. It's just the other side of the village. But I really don't . . .'

'Oh, I'm not needed here. Claire's still sitting up with Dickie, reading him stories. I don't think she'll be down for dinner even.' He could not help sounding resentful at the continuing exclusion. Driving to the convent would keep him occupied, thought Nan. She felt triumphantly unselfish, she would have so much preferred to be alone.

'Thank you. I'd be so grateful,' she said.

As they swept down the hill in Prescott's Rover they passed another car ascending.

'Pre-war,' announced Prescott. 'Tied up with string by the sound of it.'

'That was Dr Fortuno,' admitted Nan.

There was a sudden silence, in which the smell of the hot afternoon and the unspoken thoughts of two suspicious adults mingled somehow inextricably, so that ever afterwards a certain sour breath of coming storm would bring back to Nan that uncomfortable moment, the knowledge that as she and Prescott hurried to her interview with Sister Angela so at the same time Fortuno bent over the hand of Prescott's wife.

'I didn't have to charm her,' he said afterwards in answer to Nan's accusation. 'She just came to me.'

'Like the birds to St Francis?' suggested Nan acidly.

Now: 'You know, I'm not sure he's ill at all,' said Prescott as they entered the village. 'Dickie, I mean. He looks all right to me. He keeps asking to get up.'

'Dr Fortuno is very conscientious,' and Nan looked studiously out of the window. 'He's a good doctor.'

The heat was oppressive. There was a sudden roll of thunder and a few drops of rain. Has Fortuno a conscience when it comes to married women? wondered Nan. Maria had said he had a satyr's face, but there had never been a whisper of scandal, though there were plenty of women in the village who invented illness in the hope that one day he might look at them with less than professional concern. But . . . he climbed the stairs this morning like a young man, she remembered. He said to me, 'Anna, she's not only beautiful, she's *simpatica*.'

'Which road?' asked Prescott.

'Turn left.'

Large raindrops spattered the windscreen, stopped, drummed down again furiously. Alan Prescott craned to see the road.

'Some holiday!' he said.

68

7

THE convent stood back from the road behind a wall. The stone was crumbling after five hundred years of neglect, yet there still seemed, to Nan, to be mighty defences.

'Signora Mortimer,' she said through the grille. A key grated in the ancient lock.

Then there was a courtyard to cross.

'What rain!' cried the young nun in whose footsteps she hurried.

It's all right for you, thought Nan uncharitably. The nuns wore layer upon modest layer. She could feel the water trickling between her breasts, down her back. Her dress clung between her thighs.

They passed through another door. All the doors were massive and took effort to open and close. There was a corridor, white, with a heavily beamed ceiling. Nothing could be more Puritan, thought Nan. At the far end, near the door to Sister Angela's office, hung the crucifix, gruesome in its realism, and beside it on a plinth a statue of Mary holding out loving and imploring arms. Beneath on a great medieval chest, polished as only nuns and sailors know how, stood a bowl of roses.

Left here to contemplate, Nan shivered. The smell of stone, wood, polish, roses, overpowered her. There was nothing to sit on, no pictures to look at, only the uncompromising cross, the plaster woman with her open arms. In the silence, as a background to silence, there was the distant tap of good solid shoes on tile, low voices, the ringing of a pan set down, a dish taken up. Somewhere near, behind another of the doors, was a kitchen or refectory. But I've forgotten which one, thought Nan.

'Signora, how are you?' Sister Angela was a small square woman with delicate hands unfolding from beneath her scapular to grasp both of Nan's.

'There's a storm,' Nan said unnecessarily.

Sister Angela chafed her damp skin. 'You ought to change. But I'm not sure what I can offer you. I'll ring for Sister Andrea.'

'Please don't. I'm quite all right.'

They passed into the office. How quiet it always is, Nan thought. In such quiet it was difficult to imagine forty orphans spoiling for pillow fights.

Sister Angela was looking at Nan's dress, the damp tendrils of hair, the drops she wiped surreptitiously from her neck.

'I think we must get straight to the point,' she said ominously.

I feel exhausted, thought Nan. The young nun who showed her out was not the young nun who had showed her in but wore the same expression of inner certainty.

'Good night, signora,' she said softly as the gate

swung open as if sympathetically aware of Nan's
turmoil.

'And how was Reverend Mother or whatever she's
called?' asked Alan Prescott.

'Like an amiable dragon, all smiles over the smoulder.
I sat like a schoolgirl with my hands in my lap
and simply nodded at everything she said, a perfect
coward.'

'I hope it wasn't anything serious.'

Nan made no reply, gazed out into the dark. 'How
late it is. I'm sorry you had to wait so long.'

'Oh, Claire won't have missed me.'

No, thought Nan wearily, I don't suppose she has.

Maria had gone to bed. The kitchen was warm and
empty. Even so, electrical charges lingered on the air.
Nan sat at the table with a glass of wine.

'Anna?'

'Is somebody ill?' It was an automatic enquiry.

'No, nobody ill. I've been up to see the boy.'

'At midnight?'

'His temperature rose after dinner. Mrs Prescott was
frightened.'

'Was she? Nobody told me.' Nan sank back and
picked up her wine. She had been ready to recoil from
further crises and it was simply Fortuno making a fool
of himself over a pretty woman. 'You know there's
nothing wrong with him.'

He looked at the bottle, the glass, at her. 'Is anything
the matter?'

'Oh, I suppose . . . Drowning my sorrows,' she said,
and gave a small uncertain laugh and drank deeply. 'I
spent a gruelling hour with Sister Angela. She gave me
a lecture on chastity. I believe she thinks it's my fault

Graziella and Don Michele are in love. She quoted several popes, a bishop and a few saints for good measure. I don't know how they were connected. But she was adamant on Perugia.'

After a while: 'She means well, poor woman,' said Fortuno.

Nan ignored this. 'And then there's Molly Baghot. After dinner she spent half an hour telling me about her son in the Royal Flying Corps.'

'In what?'

'It all happened forty years ago. She talked as if it was yesterday. I'm sure he's dead. I'm sure he was killed in France.'

'Well, he didn't come to his father's funeral.'

'No, and the solicitor's never mentioned him. I just can't bring myself to ask her, not when she talks as if he'll come through the door at any moment.'

Fortuno came to sit opposite. 'She's old and lonely and confused. What was her life like with the old man?'

'I don't know.'

'Perhaps not very happy.'

Nan was thinking: But I've run out of patience. And pity. Time means nothing to her, or other people's inconvenience. She's like a child expecting everything to time: meals, bath, bed . . . She never asks who pays or dreams that she might outstay her welcome.

'Anna?'

Nan had put her head down on her arms and her loose hair spread over the table. For a moment Fortuno thought she was crying, but when he leaned across the table to touch her shoulder he found she was asleep.

It had begun with the Major dying in Robin's bed, thought Nan, and was somehow continuing with the

72

child who now occupied it. The world had tilted. 'We're all askew,' she wrote to Aunt Dot, but could not explain herself. Instead she added, 'And I think Dr Fortuno is in love.'

'I can't fault him,' said Alan Prescott, coming to her sitting-room after breakfast. 'But he's always here. There's his fee to consider, isn't there?' He dug his hands into his pockets, embarrassed. 'I don't mean I grudge the money. I wouldn't like you to think . . . Of course not . . . Only . . .'

'You'd like to stay another two nights.' She felt compelled to help him from his quagmire. She opened the bookings ledger and fussed unnecessarily with the pages.

'Can you manage it? I'd be so grateful. Claire doesn't want Dickie to travel so soon after . . . after whatever it was.'

No, I can't manage two more nights, Nan thought. I've already told Molly Baghot I'm fully booked after Friday. An inner voice said softly: But Molly will be gone on Friday so you won't be caught out in the lie.

'Yes, I can do that,' she said.

'And the doctor . . .'

'I'll ask him for his account.'

When she followed him out she saw that Claire Prescott was on the terrace drinking coffee. Even from a distance she looked endearingly fragile, her pale hair tied back. She also had about her, Nan knew, the indefinable air of a woman wooed.

'I expect he kisses her hand,' said Maria, giving a demonstration on her own podgy fingers, though implicit in her swift glance at Nan was the knowledge of how erotic such kisses might be.

'The doctor?' Nan feigned innocence, busying herself

73

with the bread receipts. 'These bills were all cleared,' she said, distracted. 'Is all this extra?'

'Picnics. And you'll have to do something about that girl.' Apparently she had discovered Graziella stealing writing paper.

'It's all a fuss about nothing,' insisted Nan. 'One sheet. One envelope. I'd have given it to her if she'd asked.'

'Stealing is stealing,' declared Maria.

'All the same . . .'

'She stole them to write a love letter.' There was no playfulness now, no kissing of fingers. Maria looked implacable. 'A love letter to a priest! Holy Mary, what's the world coming to?'

'I don't suppose it's much worse than it ever was. What about Eloise and . . .' Nan suddenly remembered the outcome. 'We don't choose the people we love, Maria.'

'She ought to be sent away.'

'Father Emilio and Sister Angela are busy arranging it. And no one listens to me. I happen to like Graziella. If there has to be any sending away why not send both?'

'Both?'

'Why the assumption that Graziella is the temptress?'

'She's a little whore,' said Maria.

'I won't have you calling her that.'

'But, signora . . .'

'Go away.'

Going away meant leaving the kitchen. It was an unprecedented order. Maria remained where she was, swaying a little. 'Signora?'

'Maria, go away.'

It was like this the rest of the morning. Nan picked the vegetables without consulting Antonio and when he hurried after her to remonstrate she cut him short with, 'I think you should plant more beans.'

'She's in a mood,' he reported at the back door.

'Don't we know it,' said Maria.

Nan often exasperated them by indecision but she rarely had fits of temper, was rarely obstinate. 'Obdurate,' Aunt Dot would have preferred. 'But she knows how,' she would have added. After Robin's death the villa had been turned inside out. They had all seen how difficult, how demanding Nan could be. Today she burned into the kitchen at noon, just when Maria had thought it safe to take full control in her kingdom again, and said, 'The Prescott child's howling and howling upstairs. Where's Mrs Prescott?'

'I don't know, signora.'

'She was on the terrace earlier.'

'She was on the terrace until Dr Fortuno arrived.'

'Then where's Mr Prescott?'

'He drove off to Assisi.'

'By himself, poor man,' remarked Giuseppina from the sink.

In the hall the sound of the child crying was unbearable. Nan ran up the stairs and opened the door of his room.

'I want Mummy,' he sobbed at her. His hair was damp, his face red and puffy from prolonged grief. In a sudden rush of anxiety, exasperation, energy, Nan gathered him to her, smoothing the burning forehead and pushing back the spikes of hair.

'Mummy's in the garden. We'll go and find her.'

He made no protest at being handled by a stranger. He submitted himself to the cold flannel, turning up his face obediently. She bundled him into his small dressing-gown and led him to the door. Had his temperature subsided along with his crying? He looked more normal now, infused with excitement at the adventure. He clasped her hand tightly and on the stairs he pulled her a little, going in front.

They went out by way of the kitchen because Nan had forgotten something.

'No fish? But, signora, why no fish?'

'I can't remember. I didn't listen to the excuses.'

'Signora, what am I to do without the fish?'

'I'm sure you'll think of something,' said Nan.

In a moment unbridled passion might have taken over, the fishmonger dismembered verbally, his past and future fish execrated. But: 'Dickie!' breathed Giuseppina, bending down, and Maria's face smoothed from wrath to joy. They fell on him with cries of welcome and sympathy combined. They gave him fresh lemonade and kissed him and stroked his drying hair. He suffered everything with a remarkable calm, enchanted by the novelty. Nan's only contribution was to feel his forehead. It was dry and warm, perfectly normal. How quickly the young revive, she thought. It was like giving water to a flower: effects were almost instantaneous.

Out in the garden they made a detour to see the hens. As they stood looking, a laugh surprised them on the still air.

'That's Mummy,' said Dickie, unconcerned. It was as if he had entirely forgotten all his great urgency to find her.

At last Nan prised him from the hens. 'Come on,' she commanded. He came on, but reluctantly, turning several times to look back.

There was heat and silence. Claire Prescott did not laugh again. Perhaps she's being kissed, thought Nan, and not on her hand. She and Dickie walked softly between the hedges on the paths that had once been gravel. Where the formal garden ended and they could see the meadow, Dickie hesitated, dragging at her skirt.

'There's Mummy.'

Too close for strangers, not close enough for lovers, Nan thought, shading her eyes. Slowly she walked down towards them.

'Dickie was bored. I thought some fresh air wouldn't hurt him.' Nan thought she caught a glint of humour in Fortuno's eye. 'He was calling for you,' she told Claire.

'Oh Dickie.' The girl was a delightful pink. Her eyes avoided Nan's.

'We've seen the hens,' announced Dickie, afraid she would carry him back to bed. 'Come and see the hens, Mummy.'

'How lovely, darling. He looks so much better, doesn't he?' and she appealed to Fortuno, smiling, more deeply pink.

Fortuno looked over her head at Nan. 'Mrs Baghot and Don Michele have been talking under the cherry tree.'

'Have they? Perhaps Molly's taken on the role of Juliet's nurse.'

She saw his blank look. Dickie pulled gently at her hand. 'Can *we* go to the cherry tree?'

'Yes, let's,' and she walked on while he swung on her arm grinning, stumbling now and then on the skirt of his dressing-gown. They left the hedges and the paths and the urns and the rose bower and went down the wild pulsating meadow where little lizards ran from underfoot.

Under the cherry tree Molly Baghot sat all alone, her hands folded in her lap, her eyes closed.

★

'Your son,' said Nan. 'What happened to him?'

They were all three under the cherry tree and Molly was drawing pigs with curly tails for Dickie, who lay enraptured at her feet.

'We had such fun, the two of us,' and Molly handed over another page: 'That's Auntie Pig.'

'Do Uncle Pig,' commanded Dickie.

'That was when he was little of course,' Molly continued, only pausing in her drawing to remove her hat which was so uncomfortable and had left a deep red line across her forehead. 'He didn't come back from France. Crashed. Edward said . . . Edward read the telegram.'

'I'm sorry.'

'Not this last war. Oh, years ago. But he's still with me. Sometimes he's with me all day as if he never went away. A lovely boy.'

'You said *I* was a lovely boy,' protested Dickie.

'And so you are. Shall I give Uncle Pig a moustache?'

'Did Edward have a moustache?'

'I'm afraid he did.'

'I haven't got one,' and Dickie rubbed his tender skin as if it still pricked from hairy kisses.

'Bobs,' said Molly as her pencil dashed away across the paper, 'was tall and dark and very shy.'

'I'm sorry,' said Nan again.

'Did Bobs have a moustache?' asked Dickie.

'No, dear. Look, here's Henrietta Pig.'

'But you've done three little ones.'

'They must be her children.'

Dickie had discarded his dressing-gown. The two women took no notice. They did not exclaim and force him to put it on again, telling him he would catch cold. They obviously knew it was far too hot for anyone to catch cold. The younger one was lying back, her arms

78

flung out, her shoes kicked off. The old one said, 'There, a whole family of pigs.'

'There's someone calling,' murmured Nan. Her bad temper ran from her into the hard earth under her shoulders.

'Ignore them,' said Molly. 'Can't we siesta out here?'

'Can I siesta?' asked Dickie.

'It's your mummy,' Nan told him. 'I expect she wants to give you lunch.'

Dickie made himself small, sinking down in the circle of Molly's frail arm. 'I don't want lunch. It's always that pudding.'

'Macaroni,' said Nan, who had watched Claire Prescott showing Maria how to make it. When she had gone Maria had cried, 'Milk, sugar ... Food for hyenas. The child needs meat to make him strong.'

'She's gone,' said Molly, listening.

For a long time after that there were only the small noises of their immediate world: insects, small birds in the cherry branches, the rustling of the grass. Dickie fell asleep. Nan dozed, now and then brushing away the small flies. From some deep pool of peace she rose at last, clutching as she did so at the other question she had wanted to ask.

'How's Father Michele? Is he better?'

Molly made no reply. When Nan finally opened her eyes and looked she saw that the wrinkled mauve lids were tightly shut, that the tiny hands with their slender bones and prominent veins were folded round Dickie and a lapful of paper pigs.

'I'm fast asleep, dear,' said Molly.

8

MRS Holland was gathering her bearers for an expedition to Assisi. The front steps were strewn with bags.

'So kind of Mr Prescott to offer to take us,' Miss Elwes whispered to Nan. She was rather nervous, expecting to be crushed, both by the force of Mrs Holland's personality and physically by the young honeymoon couple with whom she would have to share the back seat.

'I hope they have the sense to run away by themselves as soon as they reach the town,' Nan said to Maria as they watched the car pull away down the drive, but she thought they were probably in for a day of relentless sightseeing. They seemed already disenchanted with each other and inclined to cling to the company of others. 'Perhaps he isn't much of a lover,' said Maria. Her tone suggested it was only to be expected. 'The English are all strange,' she added, but only as she turned away, so that Nan might not hear.

Nan had only just come back from taking Molly

Baghot to Signora Falcone's. This had been necessitated by a further telegram asking Molly not to arrive before Wednesday of the following week, signed Ruddock.

'You'll be quite all right in the village,' Nan had said, putting Molly's cases in the Morris. 'It's a lovely old house, just opposite the bakery. If you like you can come back here for dinner. We could organize some sort of transport.'

'Oh, I'll walk,' Molly had declared.

'That Signora Falcone,' said Maria. 'Do you know how mean she is? Never changes the sheets. Charges for hot water.'

'Don't be silly,' retorted Nan.

'How could you send the old woman there?'

'There is nowhere else. Anyway, I've never heard any complaints.'

'Holy Mary, the convent would have taken her in.'

'I must admit I never thought of that,' said Nan.

'So I drove Molly to Signora Falcone's and in spite of everything that Maria said it all seemed as clean and decent as ever, an antique iron bedstead and holy pictures and a window overlooking the square,' Nan wrote to Aunt Dot. 'Molly seemed delighted, which was a relief, as she had cried after breakfast and I'd almost relented and turned out the attics for her. Afterwards I called at Dr Fortuno's to ask if he'd bring her up to the villa when he came to visit Claire Prescott about seven o'clock. Do you remember his house? Tall, seventeenth-century I suppose, seen better times. It's in the Piazza Antica, that tiny little square behind the church.'

Nan had never entered the house before.

'The doctor will be a moment, signora,' said the house-keeper.

The inevitably raucous sounds of Cittavigile did not penetrate. There was not even the ticking of a clock. Nan wandered aimlessly, picked up books, put them down, moved a shutter to see, astonished, a small formal garden between high walls. Everything was old and shabby and much used and had once been beautiful: the wood she touched, the binding of the books, the silk cushions.

'I never imagined . . .' she began as Fortuno came into the room, and then stopped. She had nearly said, 'I never imagined that you lived like this, alone and in such faded splendour.'

'What a delightful surprise,' he said, though she thought she glimpsed a fleeting mockery in his expression.

'I came to ask a favour.'

The housekeeper brought coffee, so strong Nan's heart raced. Ordinary conversation seemed difficult. The dim silence of the room depressed talk. Fortuno's watchfulness, keeping his distance over by the window, made the words die in her throat. She felt slightly dizzy.

'How strange I've never visited you before,' she said at last, having nothing else left.

'I never invited you. In a village there's always so much gossip.'

It had never occurred to her that he might need to be circumspect on her account. Or on his own. In case Cittavigile might think he was making love to the English widow? She grew hotter than before, and dizzier.

'How sad,' she said lightly. 'How can people be friends if their every meeting might give rise to silly speculation?'

'They must meet in public.'

'In the square, you mean?' She would have like to laugh but her heart seemed unable to cope with extra effort.

'At the Villa Giulia, for instance, where there are guests and the girls, Maria, Antonio . . .'

'Yes, of course.'

'We're old-fashioned in the country,' he remarked quietly. She suspected that he was laughing at her.

'I must go,' she said, rising.

He opened the door for her. The housekeeper was in the hall. Listening? wondered Nan.

'You won't forget Molly Baghot?'

'I'll call for her at seven.'

She put out her hand with formal politeness. His clasp was hard and impersonal. They might have just come from a medical consultation.

'After that,' she wrote to Aunt Dot, 'I had to see the butcher, a monthly interview I hate, but I can't send Maria because she swears he sends us scrag ends and there'd be a row of apocalyptic proportions among all those knives and cleavers. I tottered along to his shop on legs that seemed quite uncontrollable, not mine at all, the effect of Dr Fortuno's excessively strong coffee. The butcher was so concerned he sat me down and gave me iced water and then something "to restore the circulation". It tasted homemade and certainly got at my circulation but not in any way that reversed the effect of the coffee. I don't remember anything of the drive home and when I reached the house Maria took one look and cried, "Holy Mother, an accident!" and ran for the brandy. Then she told me that Antonio had hurt his foot, Giuseppina was wearing fancy earrings – where had she got them? – Graziella was being rude and the telephone had never stopped ringing: we were booked up for the whole of July.'

Letters tell everything or nothing, thought Nan.

Alan Prescott arrived back from Assisi at six.

'Such a long hot day,' Miss Elwes said to Nan. 'But so interesting.'

There was a general lack of animation. The honeymoon couple were carefully ignoring each other. Mrs Holland had apparently lost her guidebook and all the postcards she had bought and efficiently written out and addressed at the lunch table. Not a success then, thought Nan. She thought too that Alan Prescott might be less than pleased to find Dr Fortuno expected at seven thirty.

'They're arguing,' said Maria.

'How do you know?'

'Go on to the terrace. You can hear them.'

'I'll do no such thing.'

'Well,' said Maria, 'if he's any kind of man he'll say it has to stop.'

Half an hour later the Prescotts came downstairs. Could Nan listen for Dickie? He was nearly asleep already. They were driving down to the village for a drink; it would make a change and Claire had been in the villa all day. Claire looked pale and tearful. Her eyes fixed on Nan's desperately as if Nan might be expected to understand, to do something. She was dressed for dinner in a white dress with a very tight waist and a full skirt.

'How these fashions suit the young,' remarked Miss Elwes, watching them go out of the door.

'Such a pretty child,' said Mrs Holland, but without approval.

'She'll be disappointed,' said Maria when Nan returned to the kitchen. 'She'll be kept out till dinner and after that he'll take her up to bed.'

'Mr Prescott is still in the small single,' Nan replied as if that might be a consideration.

Maria raised her eyebrows. 'Pina says the child's been moved back. Signor Prescott insisted.'

But it was seven thirty and Molly ran in like a girl to recount her several startling conversations with Signora Falcone whose English was confined to a dozen words and whose Italian Molly rarely understood. Nan was reduced to saying helplessly 'I'm sure that can't be true,' or 'No, I'm sure she was happily married,' and 'It can't be her daughter, she only had sons.'

'Well, it's all very interesting,' Molly finished. 'Don't you think people are interesting, dear?'

'What's happened to Dr Fortuno?'

'I think he's in the garden.'

Nan retired to her sitting-room. She must bring the books up to date and finish the letter to Aunt Dot. She thought of Molly in the dining-room, laughing, holding court. How happy she is, she thought, and tried not to be astonished. What had she suffered with the Major to make her so glad to have lost him?

Fortuno asked, 'Are you busy?'

'Not yet. Come in.'

He came in but did not sit, preferring to stroll about looking at her pictures, her few photographs. He asked disconcertingly, 'Is this really you?'

'It was me. My wedding day.'

'You don't look . . .' but he broke off as if conscious of committing an unkindness. When Nan picked up the photo later she found that the thin young face it showed was certainly strained and bleak as if, instead of being married, it had received bad news.

Fortuno had already lifted the smallest picture, one of a child on a swing.

85

'You again? You look startled.'

'I probably was. Photography was considered frivolous in my house and my mother frowned on frivolity.'

'Did your husband?'

'What an odd question,' and her face wrinkled up like a puzzled child's. 'I don't think he did. I don't think we ever had enough money to be frivolous.'

'Is money absolutely necessary?'

'I suppose not.'

'You never danced? You never went to the festivals?'

'No.'

She watched him still brooding over the child on the swing as if trying to understand by what process she had become the woman behind him, sitting defensively at her desk full of ledgers.

'Do you blame me for making love to her, Anna?'

'Claire Prescott? It's none of my business.'

'You disapprove.'

'She's a married woman.'

'I didn't have to charm her. She just came to me.'

'Like the birds to St Francis?'

'I meant no harm.'

'But you've made her love you.'

'It isn't love.'

Love and sex sometimes grow muddled in women's minds, Nan wanted to say, especially young women without much experience of either. Whatever you meant, how can you tell what harm you might not do?

'There's the gong for dinner. Will you stay?'

He shook his head. 'I've work to do.'

'P.S.' Nan wrote on Aunt Dot's letter. 'Dr Fortuno only stayed twenty minutes and Giuseppina said Claire Prescott had been crying.'

*

Sister Angela sent another emissary.

'A nun on a bicycle is an arresting sight,' remarked Molly, watching Sister Perpetua dismount. She had been playing marbles on the front step with Dickie.

'I expect she's come to give me Graziella's notice,' said Nan, and afterwards: 'What did I tell you? A fortnight.'

'But there'll be handsome young men in Perugia.'

'Plenty, one hopes. But not Father Michele.'

'It's so sad,' said Molly.

'Being happy seems to cause such inconvenience, doesn't it?'

'My dear, you sound quite bitter.'

Maria, slicing tomatoes, said, 'Dr Fortuno has called again. He's gone to the vegetable garden.'

'*Where?*' asked Nan.

'The vegetable garden.'

'But why?'

'Mrs Prescott took the little boy to see the hens.'

'But Antonio will be there.'

Maria grinned. 'A man can close his eyes,' she said.

Nan got up early and walked to the meadow. Already the sky was the palest blue. She remembered Robin striding down to the wall and stopping to look back at her.

'We could have a tennis court if you like,' he had said.

'We haven't the money. Besides, I like it rough grass and flowers.'

And besides that, there was the view. 'You couldn't play tennis with that view to distract you,' she said.

'I don't see why not. You wouldn't notice it if you were concentrating on hitting the ball.'

Nan had felt herself wanting in such dedication. She soon tired of tennis balls. 'Views like that should be looked at,' she asserted.

'Then anyone living in a beautiful place would never get any work done.'

'Most work might turn out to be unnecessary.'

'You do know you're talking nonsense? Still, we could have a seat here instead, I suppose.'

There was no seat. When she came here alone Nan sat on the wall, dangling her legs like a child. This morning she stared across the valley and thought again of her desperate cry to Robin: 'I wouldn't know how to live in such a place.'

The air was so clear. She could smell the cypresses, the crushed damp grass where she had walked, the stones. A sense of unreality moved in her. Though there were landmarks she no longer recognized them. The country was strange to her.

'How sad you look,' remarked Father Emilio, dismounting from his bicycle.

'You're about early.'

'There is an old man dying at San Sulpice.'

He came to stand by the wall, the bicycle leaning against his hip. Dew and dust wreathed the hem of his cassock.

'How is Don Michele?' Nan was moved to ask.

'His head is better,' was the cautious reply.

'And his heart?'

Father Emilio banged his hat against his knee as if to extract imaginary dust. 'How romantic you are, signora.'

'Well, I suppose that having fallen in love people don't fall out of it overnight.'

'Oh, love. I thought we were talking about sexual attraction. Only a romantic would confuse the two.'

'Are they never confused then? When you marry people in your church don't you assume they love and desire together?'

Father Emilio shifted his bicycle. He was angry, she could see. Good, she thought. He ought to be angry, sensibly, humanly angry. He ought to rage on Father Michele's behalf, on Graziella's.

'Don Michele,' he began, surprisingly calmly since his eyes were hot under their belligerent brows. 'Don Michele wants to remain a priest.'

Nan waited, but the statement was, apparently, intended to say everything.

'But he wants Graziella,' she pointed out.

'He cannot have her and remain a priest. Therefore he will give her up. He is resigned to it. He has told me so.'

He would tell you anything, Nan thought. So would I if you put me on the rack where you put him. She remembered how she had parried his questions after the incident in the meadow. But I was ignorant then, she thought, and ignorance made me brave. Poor Father Michele. She thought of his hair springing under her searching hand, the white young face. 'You're too soft,' Robin had said. 'You can't save the world.' At the time she had been nursing a swallow in the cup of her hand, a stunned baby, its eyes closed. 'You can't put it back in the nest,' he had told her. 'Just leave it. It might live or . . .'

'Or for want of a little help it might die.'

'But what kind of help can you give it?' asked Robin.

'So Don Michele's chosen,' she said quietly. The sun had driven away the last of the mist; all the pearly coolness was lost.

'He says so. And he's sorry for such foolishness.'

89

'I don't think love is foolishness,' and then, seeing his expression: 'Oh, I know. I know. It wasn't love.'

They stood for a moment in prickly animosity.

Then she felt compelled to ask, 'Didn't you ever feel what he's feeling? Didn't you ever . . .'

'Never.'

'Then you're a liar,' cried Nan, and slid off the wall and strode away up the meadow, head down, while Father Emilio called after her.

After a while he stopped calling, and went on his way to San Sulpice.

'I shouldn't have told him he was a liar,' Nan wrote to Aunt Dot, reopening her letter. 'I haven't done Protestants or Englishwomen anywhere any good. I've simply confirmed him in all his prejudices. Perhaps he'll never drink wine with me again.'

'How hot you look, dear,' Molly had said as she had run into the hall.

'Hot? Oh, I've been down on the meadow and had to hurry back. It's so late. I hadn't realized . . . But why are you here? Has something happened?'

'I don't think so,' and Molly looked a little doubtful, as if something might have happened which she had forgotten. 'I think it was just the smell from the bakery. It wakes me early. And I thought I'd like to walk up to see you.'

'It's not breakfast-time yet. What will Signora Falcone think?'

'Your breakfasts are better than hers, dear. You won't mind if I sit under the vine and look at the garden, will you?'

'What can I do?' Nan asked Maria, pouring coffee in the kitchen. 'Should I ring Signora Falcone? I never expected her to walk all the way up here for breakfast.'

'Drink,' commanded Maria, handing her the cup. 'Don't worry. What does Signora Falcone matter? And the old lady is a little mad. How many times have we said it?'

'I can't help wondering what sort of future she'll have. She can't stand this Lily. What did you mean the other day when you said she was cruel?'

'Ever since a child.'

'Cruel?'

'Spoiled. The favourite. Oh, the tales . . .'

When have you had time to listen to Molly's tales? Nan wondered. She could hear the growl of the Morris, doors slamming. 'I've told them and told them to be quiet,' she exclaimed. 'What will the guests think?'

But Miss Elwes was already up, her knitting bag on her arm. 'The best time of day,' she told Nan. 'I can sit undisturbed. My niece has had a baby, you know.' She pulled out some minuscule garments, sugary pink.

'Are you picnicking again?' Nan enquired.

'I hope so. Is it a bother, Mrs Mortimer? I know you don't do lunches.'

'Occasional picnics are no trouble but this last week everyone has wanted sandwiches and boiled eggs.'

'How very English.'

'It's not only the English. The French picnic too.'

'On boiled eggs?'

By this time they had reached the terrace. Molly looked as small as a child on the wicker lounger, her little feet in their high-quality sensible old-fashioned shoes decorously, tightly together.

'What luxury!' exclaimed Miss Elwes doubtfully. She found Molly unsettling and already, before she had extracted her needles, anticipated dropping stitches.

'Mrs Prescott is up already and has gone to the cherry tree,' remarked Molly.

'Is there a cherry tree?' asked Miss Elwes. 'I haven't seen one.'

Nan automatically glanced away towards the meadow, though the hedges cut off the view.

'I expect,' continued Molly mysteriously, 'he kisses her palm and her ears and the nape of her neck. I can't imagine her husband doing any of those, can you? Some men only bother with the obvious.'

Nan opened her mouth and closed it again.

'You still look hot, dear. Is anything wrong?'

'I'm rather glad I don't know what you're talking about,' said Miss Elwes, shying away.

'It's going to be a rather busy day, that's all,' said Nan.

After breakfast Nan found Claire Prescott on the stone seat and told her that her husband was looking for her, he wanted to start for Gubbio.

'But I don't want to go.'

'I'm afraid he doesn't seem in a very good mood,' said Nan.

'He's being so unreasonable. After all, we leave the day after tomorrow. We could look at Gubbio on the way to Florence – and I really don't care about either. And Dickie's always sick in the car.'

Nan leaned to brush a piece of grass from the girl's shoulder.

'He didn't come,' was the anguished whisper.

'Did he say he would?' asked Nan sensibly. She talks to me, she thought, as if in our few conversations, perhaps half a dozen sentences, we had grown as close as women can.

'No. No, he didn't. He said he sometimes drove past on the back road in the mornings. He has a patient up at . . . up at some farm. I thought if I sat in the meadow . . .' She leaned suddenly against Nan's arm. She was weary with longing, wearier still with the growing knowledge that the longing would remain unfulfilled. And Nan thought: Other people's confidences are intolerable burdens but how are we to repudiate them? The sad weight of the girl's head reproached her for even trying and she moved it gently, stroking back the hair.

'It'll be all right,' she offered.

'How can it be?' Claire challenged. She knew she would walk round Gubbio all day sullen with this new ripeness, this inner heat, this excruciating sensitivity, while her husband talked to her of Ottaviano Nelli and Dickie, bored to death, swung irritatingly on her arm.

Nan, severely practical, lent her a handkerchief.

'I can hear them calling,' she said.

Back at the house they had called a long time but then been distracted by Dickie howling that he didn't like cars, he didn't, he didn't . . . He kept this up on a rising note until Claire ran up to him and flung her arms about him. It was not the first time Nan had watched a child accumulate attention from those who, the moment before, were participating in adult tragedies. In pacifying him both Prescotts abandoned their preoccupations and so diminished them.

'What holy peace,' said Maria. 'Have they gone?'

'At last.'

'Thank God. Now we can get back to normal.'

9

HE lay flat on the warm earth, his eyes closed.

'The wrong woman,' he said. 'I should have known.'

'Yes, you should,' agreed Nan. She had her back to the trunk of the cherry and now and again she tried opening her eyes but the landscape remained a blur of coloured light. 'It *is* my meadow,' she added some minutes later. 'You might have expected me to be sitting in it.'

He had left his car below, had climbed the wall, had hurried up the slope. She had watched him with interest, realizing his mistake. She knew that in her flowered dress and straw hat she was just a woman reading a book in the shade: any woman. He had come quite close before he knew she was not the woman he most wanted to see.

'Is nobody ill today?' she asked. 'What have you done with your patients?'

'I have a surgery this evening. What have you done with your guests?'

'They're out, every last one. The Prescotts have gone

to Gubbio. Mrs Holland has taken poor Miss Elwes by bus to some hermitage in the mountains. And Molly Baghot . . .'

'Ah,' said Fortuno. 'Molly Baghot.'

'I don't know what to do about Molly.'

'I thought you didn't.'

'The latest plan is for her to catch a train next Tuesday – but I don't suppose she will. It'll be put off till Thursday and then maybe the following Monday and on and on.' She was amazed that she could speak of it and smile.

'Isn't she happy with Signora Falcone?' His words had long pauses between. Was he going to sleep?

'But who . . .' Nan began. Who is to pay the bills? she had been going to say. A week, two weeks . . . Was it now to be the whole summer? I'm feeding her for nothing, she could have added, for she knew she would never charge in spite of Degnare's grumbling: '*Everything* must be written down, signora. Everything. We shall claim from the estate of the late Major.'

She squinted down at Fortuno's dark head. Grey hairs, she thought, and I never noticed them before.

'What are you thinking?' he asked, though his eyes did not open.

'A punt on the Cam,' she said but in Italian, for his sake, it came out: 'A boat on a river.'

'Long ago?'

'Years and years. Before my father died. Before I was eighteen.' The water had run down the pole, bright drops scattered on the worn cushions. Under the overhanging trees the stirred mud gave off the sour smell of decay. The boy's kiss had been less clumsy than expected, but then he had practised elsewhere. She had been made breathless by the sensation and the promise.

He had said 'Please' and 'Let me' and 'Like this', the usual things. But I hadn't heard them before, thought Nan afterwards. Evelyn, alerted, had asked, 'What have you been doing together?' and something that might have been beautiful disintegrated into a mess of shame and concealment and recrimination.

Robin had loved her and been kind but in bed had been silent and almost disinterested. He would have preferred, Nan thought, simply to be her friend. 'He loves his old dog better than me,' she wrote to Aunt Dot, meaning that with the dog he was more demonstrative, talking, caressing. Once she tried to explain her feelings to Robin, a miserable process which only made him anxious. He had not imagined that she could find fault. It knocked his confidence strangely. So I'd have been better keeping silent, Nan thought.

Other women accepted sex without love; welcomed it. It meant nothing or it meant physical relief, a pleasure like scratching or yawning or sinking into hot water. How ironic, Nan thought, that I have had love and hardly any pleasure.

'Now what are you thinking?'

'That we're never satisfied.'

Fortuno sat up, brushing twigs from his hair. 'Never? Not often perhaps. But has it taken you till now to realize it?'

She lifted her face to the sunlight filtering through the cherry leaves as, had there been one, she would have lifted her face for a lover's kiss.

'I'm sorry I wasn't Claire,' she said.

'On the contrary, you're glad. You see my disappointment as a moral victory. The temptation to sin has been removed to Gubbio.' He stood up as if impatient. She had never seen him discomfited before, like an uncertain and belligerent boy. Did frustrated desire reduce a sober, capable man to this?

'Only until tomorrow,' she reminded him. 'Tomorrow you may find her here. But be careful, this is a famous trysting place: Graziella and Don Michele, Molly and Dickie, even Antonio and Signora Arletti, I hear.'

'And you?' he countered. 'Who were you waiting for under the cherry?'

She blundered into the dim kitchen from the bright sun and Maria said, 'A fine afternoon to go out. That bloody Graziella's disappeared, left the vegetables, left the dishes . . .'

Nan felt a surge of sympathy for Graziella.

'Disappeared?'

'Disappeared. Gone off in a sulk, I expect. She was insufferable this morning – pert, answering back. So much for a broken heart.'

'So when did you last see her?'

'She went upstairs to put out the clean towels and didn't come down. I sent Pina up. "Find that lazy slut", I said. How long does it take anyone to carry a towel to the bathroom? And Pina came back and said there wasn't anyone upstairs, or downstairs. The house was empty. Signora, the girl has run away.'

'But where would she run?'

'Maybe she has another man down the valley. Or over by Concini's. Antonio saw her there one afternoon when she should have been here in her room. Who knows how many times she crept out after lunch? I asked Pina but she's not saying.'

'Did you shout at her?'

'I told her: "That girl will get you into real trouble one

of these days. She already makes you lie for her. What next?" Then I came to look for you, signora, but you'd gone out. Perhaps the wretched girl's with you, I thought. Perhaps you've both gone to Salvatore Umberti for the oil, or you've gone to church, or the *farmacia*. But no. Here you are but where is she? Signora, what is happening in this house?'

'Why,' asked Nan, stupefied, 'did you think I'd want to go to church?'

In the garden heat rose through the soles of her sandals and still she felt a chill. 'There's nothing to worry about,' she had told Maria. 'She's late back, that's all.' 'Late back from where?' Maria demanded. Nan, escaping, hurried between the hedges and round to the vegetables and then back to the stone seat as if she hoped to find Graziella weeping there as she had done once before. It was, after all, the most suitable place for lovers.

'She was pert, answering back,' Maria had said. Nan knew those moods well, those graceless lunges back into childhood, cheeky, provoking. But this Graziella must be reconciled somehow with the other, the young woman in love, tender, luminous with tears.

'Have you lost something, dear?' asked Molly, appearing from the direction of the meadow and coming to take her arm. 'Oh, I've had the most lovely day. Lovely. I do so like helping people to be happy.'

'Molly, what have you been doing?'

'Doing? Walking. I've walked miles. Why, what did you think? Oh, and I met Father Emilio: old bicycle, eyes like augers, no English . . . And three small girls with a donkey . . . And Signora Arletti on a scooter.'

'Nobody else?'

'I don't think so.' Molly made a great effort, as if her whole day was passing, event by small event, before an inner eye. 'No, dear, nobody. Really, it was so hot. Everyone must have been indoors.'

Does she think I can't recognize her . . . her subterfuges, thought Nan. She has a look, a sort of innocent abstraction just like a child avoiding a lie. She's been up to something.

'There's something going on,' she reported to Maria, who was preparing dinner.

'What sort of thing?'

'I don't know. I wish I did.'

'Have you seen the Signora Baghot? It can't be good for her all this walking. *That* was why the old Major died: he was worn out walking round Assisi. Round and round. *She* wouldn't notice how far it was but he had a bad heart, couldn't breathe, needed rest . . .' Maria panted herself, thinking of him. 'Where does an old woman find such energy?'

It was curious, Nan thought, how Maria vacillated between robust derision and a grudging admiration for Molly Baghot. Tonight she was inclined to be sharp because of Graziella, because of Giuseppina. 'I'm having to do everything,' was Giuseppina's complaint, and everything she did was criticized, and Maria continued to shout and reduce her to sulks and tears.

Other people were shouting now.

'Is that the Prescotts?' asked Nan. Was it to be an evening of raised voices?

'They didn't enjoy Gubbio. The little boy cried all day. The Signora caught the sun.' Maria reached for the pepper and the bowl of tarragon. 'It's no good, all this,' and she raised her eyes as if she could see through the ceiling to the scene of discord. 'He should be kind to her now. This way she only goes to cry on the doctor's chest.'

'Heart,' amended Nan. 'It would sound more poetic.' She picked up a knife. 'I ought to ring the convent.'

'They'll all be in chapel, signora.'

'I did hope Graziella would be back by now.'

'Not her. She's you know where doing you know what.'

'No, I don't know.'

Maria's chopping grew ferocious. Vegetables flew. Nan thought: I'm angry because I'm tired, but her knife sliced more and more slowly while Maria's did the opposite. Later, crossing the hall on her way to her room to change, she thought of all the other moments of upheaval in her life, for this was what she was experiencing, she had decided: an upheaval of all she thought settled and safe. How innocently we imagine, she thought, that life is only tricky at sixteen or seventeen, that afterwards we swim in calm waters, certain of our direction and unafraid of the current.

'Mrs Mortimer.' Claire Prescott was running down the stairs lightly and quietly, her lovely dress – another lovely dress, thought Nan – lifting in the draught to show the fine net beneath, the layered petticoats. 'I'd like to use the phone.'

'I'm afraid you have to use it in the hall.' She saw the girl's disappointment, her sudden anxiety. 'It's the only one.'

'What do I do? Could you show me?'

And: 'Is it a local call?' asked Nan, as if she did not know.

'She'd been crying,' said Molly. It was cool on the

terrace but she had borrowed a shawl from Maria and sat wrapped in it with only her face poking out.

'She's in love,' said Nan.

'I was once.'

'With the Major?'

'The Major was at Aldershot. John was the brother of one of my friends.' Molly's face withdrew inside the folds of shawl. 'How proper we were! It was weeks before he kissed me.'

'What happened?'

'Nothing. He was killed at St Quentin.'

It was easy to imagine Molly in love, laughing, flirtatious. Had she dressed well then, had thick dark hair held up with combs? How cruel of fate to leave the Major safe at Aldershot and send the only two men she loved to certain deaths in France.

'I married at seventeen. Edward proposed after my first dance. I really had no idea what life was about. My mother thought him so suitable.'

'But Lily didn't marry.'

'Father died when she was sixteen. Mother was already dead. She . . . escaped. She said she didn't like men. She bought a little house with her share of the money and cut off her hair and smoked cigars and kept dogs.'

'In Calne?' cried Nan, overcome by the vision.

'Not Calne then. Calne came later.' There was a pause and the shawl fell back a little. 'Edward admired her.'

'Admired Lily?'

'Yes, I was surprised at first. Then I saw . . . He'd been brought up in an army family and revered rank, went to pieces if a colonel inspected his troop and found some silly fault, a button undone, boots not polished enough. Lily treated him the way the colonels did and he was used to it, he obeyed. Fetch this, cut the cake, Edward, let the dogs out, Edward ... I thought he'd feel humiliated but you see, he'd been bullied all his life. I was the only one who couldn't make him do what I wanted,' and her voice fell away to a whisper. 'I had no rank. I was less than his worst soldier.'

'It was unkind of him to make Lily your ...'

'Keeper,' said Molly. 'He thought I couldn't fend for myself.'

'If you can't bear to live with Lily they must let you have some of the money. I'm sure of it.'

Molly shrank away within the shawl until it seemed only her hands remained, clutched together. No rings, thought Nan suddenly.

'Lily wouldn't let them. She wants it for herself.'

10

AT nine o'clock Nan felt it imperative to ring Sister Angela. In such circumstances, what did one say? There may be no need to say anything, she thought. Graziella might be at the convent this very moment telling them 'Signora Mortimer doesn't know where I am . . .'

The first time she dialled there was a fault. 'The line's always unreliable,' she had informed Aunt Dot during her stay. 'Darling, I shall never touch it again,' Aunt Dot had sworn, having called Dr Fortuno only to find herself speaking to a garage in Verona.

'I can't get through,' Nan said to Maria. Claire Prescott had no trouble an hour ago, she thought.

'Always the same. What is it? Birds on the line? Are you going to drive down, then? That wretched girl's probably back there by now and eating supper.'

'No. I shan't bother. I'll ring later.'

'Perhaps she felt ill,' suggested Giuseppina, scurrying by with dishes.

'She should have said.' Nan was stern.

'If she'd said I wouldn't have believed her,' said Maria.

Sitting in her room after dinner Nan re-read Aunt Dot's last letter. From it seemed to rise the smell of Laburnum Lodge, that remnant of Edwardian prosperity. As a child she had loved to go there. Her own home had been so modern, so comfortless – though only comfortless, she thought long afterwards, because Evelyn had made it so, not simply because of the open, public feel of the downstairs rooms. Of course, Evelyn despised Laburnum Lodge. It was cluttered with the indispensables of life before the Great War and there had been plenty of corners for absolute privacy, worn armchairs, footstools, sofas, window seats. The original range still burned in the kitchen; there were cushions embroidered long ago by ... 'By Mother!' exclaimed Evelyn. 'Dorothy, how could you?' But Dorothy could because she did not care for possessions, old, new, in fashion or out. She had never considered if she cared for the cushions any more than she had taken stock of the rest of the house or wondered whether a new gas cooker might be more convenient. Now she gazed at her mother's faultless stitching and said slowly, 'They're rather pretty really,' in a vague and offhand manner that only irritated Evelyn. 'Of course I'd never throw them out,' she reassured the young Nan later in private and Nan knew, with absolute certainty, that she would not.

'The boiler has been playing up,' wrote Aunt Dot. 'I've had Mr Fortescue in twice but he says the trouble is old age: too many years of make do and mend. He thinks it ought to be replaced. "We all have our natural span and can't be coaxed beyond it," he said ominously this morning and went on to tell me horrific tales of exploding geysers he had known in Petersfield and Petworth and even Chichester. I told him there was nothing for it, I should take to the hip bath again.'

There was the sound of sudden laughter outside in the cool dark. Molly Baghot, Nan thought. Is this what Molly was going back to: uncertain hot water, hip baths, make do and mend? Who or what was this Lily? Why should Molly, by the decision of her dead husband, be bound to live with her in Calne? 'Where?' Maria had asked, fascinated. And later: 'Is it near London?' When Nan had said, 'It's in the country. A small town,' without remembering herself how big it was, how near, far, interesting or moribund, Maria had lost interest. It might be Cittavigile in a damper climate. Presumably the Major had arranged things for the best. He must have seen Calne as a refuge for Molly, not a prison. He had known, better than anyone, that his wife was unable to fend for herself. Nan had no trouble in imagining Lily as someone who could certainly fend for herself, who had probably spent the war cultivating cabbages and making ten pounds of jam out of one pound of raspberries.

'And how is my Dr Fortuno?' Aunt Dot continued. 'What does he really think about Graziella and Father Michele? He might think Perugia offers a better life for her. You're very hard on him. He can only look at the world his way as you look at it yours . . .'

Does that mean, Nan wondered, that we are never to even glimpse each other's point of view?

'Signora, Antonio *vuol'andare* . . .' said Maria.

'Tell him to go. Tell him to ask if Graziella's there.' Nan rose, caught her breath. 'No. Maria. Tell him not to mention it.'

'The tart,' said Maria. She hung in the doorway, her scarlet face indignant. 'Have you seen the way she looks at the doctor? He'd be next best after a priest, wouldn't he?'

'Maria, shut up.'

Molly, who had been sitting quietly under the vine, only spoke when Nan walked restlessly up and down for the second time.

'Has Antonio gone? How annoying. I must have fallen asleep. Why didn't they come and fetch me?'

Nan could just make out the pale scarf at her throat.

'It's so dark. They wouldn't have guessed you were here.'

'And how is Graziella?'

'Graziella? She's missing. I expect she's just run back to the convent. She is understandably upset about Perugia.'

'But why would she go to the convent? I wouldn't, in her shoes.'

Nan sat on the stone wall and felt the hard edge press into her thighs. 'I suppose you don't know where she is?' she asked softly.

'Oh no, dear. How should I know?'

From above but distantly, for the shutters were closed, came the sound of raised voices. The Prescotts quarrelling again? thought Nan. They'll wake Dickie. Damn Fortuno. Damn Graziella.

'I must drive you to the village,' she said to Molly.

'How kind of you.'

'I only hope Signora Falcone will open her door.'

Though the greater part of Cittavigile was locked up for the night there was no problem at Signora Falcone's.

She had heard the car. 'There's no other car like it,' she said disconcertingly to Nan, who always hoped to be inconspicuous. Molly looked very small and childlike, turning to wave.

I'll sell this car, Nan was thinking, and buy something smaller, something reliable. She knew so little about cars. Could reliability be bought or was it a matter of luck? The cypresses loomed in the arc of the lights. There was a slender figure standing by the roadside. At first she thought it was a boy out after stray sheep or a strayed donkey. No one thumbed lifts on these roads even in the daytime. Then, as she drew near, she saw it was a girl, long dark hair streaming down her back.

She swerved to a halt.

'Graziella!' she cried, but the window was up, the figure stepped back from the light instinctively. 'Graziella!' and this time she had managed to open the door and was out and stumbling to the front of the car. Graziella gave a sob and ran forward.

'Signora, signora, something has happened. I know it has. I know.'

'*What* has happened?' Nan folded her in her arms. What else was she to do? The long hair blew about them both. The girl's brow was damp and hot. Her blouse was adrift from her skirt, her face wet from weeping.

Weeping? 'What has happened?' Nan asked again.

'I don't know. I don't know. He said he'd meet me and he didn't come. He would only not come if . . . if something had happened.'

'Meet you where?'

'Concini's orchard. It was always Concini's where we met after . . . after the attack in the meadow. It's away from the road up there. Isolated. A lot of them in the village don't like Michele. His father stuck to the *Fascisti* to the end. They say he betrayed partisans when he could. I don't know what's happened to him. Why didn't he come?'

'Concini's orchard.' Nan felt the slender bones tremble in the protecting curve of her arm. She's just a child, she thought, the child who sniggers at Giuseppina's crude jokes and sticks out her tongue at Maria.

'How long did you wait?'

'All afternoon. All evening. He said he'd be there at three. We . . . we were going to run away together. I had all my things with me.'

Nan had once seen all her things, the pitiful possessions of a convent orphan: a small case, a nightdress, clean knickers, toothbrush . . . 'We can afford only the bare essentials,' Sister Angela always told visitors. But for us, was the unspoken corollary, they would have nothing.

'Run away? But where would you go?'

'Michele knew somewhere. Michele . . .' She broke down again into the wretched shivering child.

Nan led her to the car. 'You'd better come back to the villa. I'll ring the convent. I'll tell them . . .' But she could not imagine what to tell them. I'll cope, she thought. This is nothing to all that fuss over the baby, the mess, the moral outrage, the recriminations. 'You mustn't worry,' she said stupidly. 'I expect he couldn't get away from Don Emilio, or somebody arrived unexpectedly, or . . .' She could not think what might detain a man from elopement.

Graziella pulled out a sodden handkerchief and wiped her face ineffectually. 'He loves me. He would have come.'

Nan wrenched the car into first gear and they climbed on slowly under the cypresses.

'Why were you on this road?' she asked. Another bend, another hundred yards and the gates would be in sight. Inside she felt she would be safe from the dark and the unreality of Graziella's anguish. She could take refuge in making coffee or hot milk or even in pouring brandy, and the rooms would be light and warm and 'normal', she thought.

'Why were you up here on this road?' she repeated. 'Nowhere near Concini's.'

'I didn't know where to go. I thought I'd come back and then I thought, no, how could I? Maria would be locking up. There's no Pina to let me in. And I couldn't go to the convent. And who else would take me in?'

They came up the drive and drew round to the courtyard. There were only two lights burning, both expected.

'Maria's in bed, thank God,' said Nan.

She rang the convent.

'Graziella isn't well,' she informed them. 'I sent her on an errand and she came back feeling . . . unwell. I've put her to bed here for the night.'

'How not well?' demanded the soft voice.

'Headache. Sickness.' That was true enough, thought Nan. Lies were slippery, untrustworthy things. But I shall have to think what on earth I could have sent her for, and Maria knows I didn't send her anywhere, and so does Giuseppina. 'Lies are always found out, Annette,' Evelyn had said. 'Did you hold this boy's hand?'

'Sister Angela's been trying to phone,' said the soft voice. 'There's been something wrong with the line.'

'I know. I tried you earlier.'

'We've been worried. Her clothes have gone, you see.'

109

'I don't know anything about clothes.'

'We thought she might have run away.'

'Why should she do that? Where could she go?'

It was a shock to return to the bedroom and 'be sympathetic', thought Nan. As she entered she wondered why she had given Graziella her own bed and not sent her to the maids' room.

'Drink this.'

'What is it?'

'Whisky and milk.'

Graziella sipped slowly, disgusted but anxious to be amenable. The bedraggled child had gone. It was a woman sitting there, one of Nan's nightdresses slipping from her shoulders. 'Where is he?' she cried. 'Why didn't he come?'

'I should sleep now,' said Nan. She removed the glass gently and set it down on the small table by the bed. 'I expect you'll find out in the morning.'

'My bag . . .'

'I'll fetch it when I can.'

Nan turned off the lamp. Graziella did not seem curious where Nan was to sleep, as if certain there must always be a spare bed for the mistress of the house. Suddenly and inexplicably exasperated Nan asked, 'Did you meet every day at Concini's?'

'Every day for a week.' This was a matter for boasting. Graziella's voice grew firmer with pride. 'Oh, but it was . . .'

Silence. A memory surfaced and fell away, like a small trout rising in a very deep pool. Nan persisted: 'And nobody knew?'

'Only . . .' The light young voice broke off, and began again more warily: 'No, no one.'

Only Molly, Nan thought. She already had her hand on the doorknob when the right question formed in her mind and she asked it, without thinking, as a small child might hook the little rising trout with a grub on the end of a string. 'Did you picnic under the trees? It's a lovely place to sit – better than the meadow.'

'Oh yes, and . . .'

Silence again.

'I should go to sleep,' Nan said. 'Tomorrow is going to be a difficult day.'

'Signora . . .' began Graziella.

But I'm tired of it all, thought Nan. 'Good night,' she said and went out. On the stairs she remembered she had not taken out a nightdress for herself.

She woke in the narrow bed in the maids' room, unused except for sudden illness and siesta. Before she remembered she was naked she had leaned from the window to look over the high wall into the vegetable garden. There's nobody to see, she thought. There were only the green rows: lettuces, beans, artichokes.

The smell of the Villa Giulia was compounded of sun-baked stone and Maria's cooking, of polish, flowers, rosemary because of the huge bushes outside, drains. Nan went down to the kitchen and let herself out into the cool morning.

Oh Molly, why did you interfere? she thought.

Sympathy ebbed from her. The sooner you go to Lily the better, she thought: the puckish child confined where she can't do any more harm. She reached the hen run and was greeted by furious clucking and cackling. They hoped she brought their breakfast.

'Signora,' said Maria as she came in through the front door and automatically swept up the fallen petals from the table. 'Don Emilio has rung. Don Michele has been out all night.'

III

'All night?'

'Don Emilio is worried.'

'Is that what he said? Or did he think I'd got Don Michele upstairs with Graziella?'

Maria looked startled. 'Upstairs, signora?'

'Did he ask about Graziella?'

'Yes, signora. I said I knew nothing.'

They looked at each other for a moment. What was she thinking when she told Father Emilio she knew nothing? wondered Nan. What if Father Emilio had been persistent?

A scuffling above made them glance upwards. Dickie was coming downstairs in his pyjamas, his hair rumpled.

'Can we go to the cherry tree?' he demanded.

I I

Nan signed the letter 'Your distracted niece'. She knew it would make Aunt Dot smile but the more she looked at it the less she smiled herself. It's true, she thought: I am distracted. And she felt almost overwhelmed by responsibility: Molly, Graziella, Father Michele, even the Prescotts. They're nothing to do with me. Why should I care what they do, how they feel? she wondered.

'Coffee, signora?' asked Giuseppina, looking in.

'Please. Is Maria in the kitchen?'

'Yes, signora.'

'The house is very quiet.'

The girl shrugged. 'There was a row over Graziella. She was late down for work.'

'I don't want to know about it.'

'It's over now. D'you want coffee here or in the *salotto*?'

The house was quiet not only because Maria was silent, podding beans with savage energy alone in the scullery. Giuseppina had tiptoed about all morning, arranging fresh flowers, polishing, closing blinds, making beds. There was no giggling with Graziella. Where was Graziella? Even Antonio, conscious of drama, kept out of the way among his vegetables. If Nan closed her eyes she could imagine that the Villa Giulia was just as it had been when Robin was alive, that all the bedrooms were empty except one. But I can't close my eyes, she thought. She needed them wide open to see her way through the minefield.

There was the convent, for instance.

'I understand you sent the girl on some errand,' said the dreaded voice.

'I can't hear a word, I'm afraid.'

'You sent the girl out somewhere. To buy something?' asked Sister Angela. The line was very bad.

'I'm sorry, I can't hear you,' said Nan.

'An errand, signora. Where did she go?'

'Graziella? To Umberti's for olive oil.'

'But they are away.' Sister Angela sounded far away in some electric blizzard. 'Signor Umberti's father died last week and they've all gone to Grosseto for the funeral.'

'I forgot about it. That's why . . . Are you there?'

'What did you say?'

'I said she's upstairs making the beds.'

'But her clothes are not here. Did Sister Xavier tell you . . .'

'I don't know anything about clothes. I'll ask her.'

In the bedroom where Mrs Holland had barely stirred the bedclothes Nan said, 'What are we going to do about your case?'

Graziella appeared indifferent. 'I don't know.'

'If I fetch it in the car can you get it into the convent without being seen?'

114

'I don't know.'

After disruption, children expect their worlds to return to being orderly, to being managed properly by those in charge. Nan said, exasperated, 'Don't forget the Prescotts leave tomorrow morning.'

'There are ways,' said Graziella, who was turned away, tucking corners. 'I can get the clothes in, perhaps not the case.'

Downstairs the letter for Aunt Dot lay on the hall table. Nan put on a hat and took up the car keys.

'Maria, I'm going to the village.'

Maria swept the beans into a pan and looked down at them morosely. 'Mr Prescott has complained there was very little hot water for his bath.'

'I think I might call on Mrs Baghot as well.'

'D'you think we need the plumber?'

Outside Antonio watched Nan wrestle with the car but did not venture near. Where she usually crashed the gears with embarrassed frustration, this morning she crashed them with determination. There was a dust cloud where she had accelerated down the drive.

'Where's she off to?' Antonio asked Maria.

'She's gone to post a letter and visit the old woman.'

'Or to scorch the tail off the devil,' said Antonio.

The case was in full view of the road. It stood forlornly on the short grass, a battered cheap cardboard object. Nan swept it up and ran back to the car, her heart beating ridiculously. Really, it was a very quiet road. Who would have noticed it? By the roadside she saw the remains of two boiled eggs.

How could you be so silly? she wanted to ask Molly. You gave them your picnics, encouraged them to meet. I expect you told them that nothing should come between lovers, not duty, common sense, nuns, vows of celibacy, pangs of hunger. So they were happy for two hours a day and will be unhappy for . . . how long? A few hours a day is something, Nan could imagine Molly replying, and more than most people have. Molly had been married to the Major at seventeen and her rare hours of happiness had been spent alone.

Nan hid the case in the boot under a tartan rug. A man with a cow on a string walked by. 'Is anything the matter, signora?'

'No. I was afraid I had a puncture.'

She climbed in and let out the clutch too fast. The car bucked and stalled. Her hands felt sweaty on the wheel. She came down the hill into Cittavigile too fast and the car coming towards her swerved abruptly, taking to the safety of the verge. It was Dr Fortuno but she did not look at him. She swept on – 'childishly' she thought. In the square she had difficulty parking because it was market day and there were stalls everywhere and loose animals.

'Isn't it fun?' said Molly. 'You can buy almost anything.'

'I thought we ought to arrange your train ticket.'

'How kind of you, dear. But I have one already.'

'Already?'

'Signora Falcone helped me.'

They sat at the café surrounded by chaotic bustle. None of the Italian women sat to drink. They were all busy. *I* should be busy, thought Nan. She was acutely aware of the case, the orphanage case, in the boot of the Morris, aware too of a black figure, tall and gaunt, somewhere on the edge of the crowd. Father Emilio. 'Like a conscience,' she said to herself.

'When are you going?' she asked Molly to take her mind off it.

'The day after tomorrow. Isn't it exciting?'

'Will Lily meet you? Or Mr Ruddock?'

'Lily? Oh, I don't think Lily . . . Why should you think she'd come all that way?'

'Molly,' and Nan put down her glass. The lemon was astringent. Her throat contracted. 'Molly, did you encourage Father Michele and Graziella to elope?'

'Did I what, dear?'

You know what. How tiresome you can be. 'Did you help them arrange to run away?'

'Have they run away then?'

'No.'

'Well then.'

There were two men leaning on the Morris. They were deep in argument. Nan stood up abruptly. 'I ought to go. Maria's upset this morning. She might murder someone.'

'But she looks so placid. Big women always seem placid.'

'Do they?'

Molly considered her. 'Bovine,' she added.

'Maria isn't bovine. What an awful word anyway.'

'You don't seem your usual self, dear,' remarked Molly sadly. 'I didn't mean to sound unkind.'

Nan picked up her bag and sorted out some loose change for the lemonade. Even this seemed an effort. She felt that her hands shook slightly, betraying the state of her nerves.

But all I did was fetch a suitcase, she thought.

Maria was singing Tosca. 'A danger signal,' Aunt Dot would have said if she'd been there to say it. Aunt Dot had come to know all Maria's repertoire and every mood and shade of mood represented in it. Nan never noticed. Only silence struck her as ominous. But at the moment Maria began on the Tosca Nan was noticing Graziella. Too many tears make even Graziella ugly, she thought.

'How will you manage?' Nan asked. She had given the girl the hideous cardboard case.

'It'll be all right,' was the quick reply. Nan detected a genuinely ruthless determination.

'But surely they'll notice?' In Nan's imagination the sisters bore down like inquisitive starlings, plucking at secrets, exposing all falsehoods.

'I'll wear all the clothes, one thing on top of another. The rest can go in my pockets. Maybe,' and she opened the lid and gazed down, undecided, 'maybe I'd better not take them all at once.'

There seemed very little there; not enough, Nan thought, for two trips. All the underwear was convent issue, white and strictly utilitarian. 'The nuns wear long vests to their knees in winter,' Giuseppina had told her once. Often the smaller orphans used them as night-gowns.

'I've told Sister Angela I sent you to Umberti's for oil.'

'But they're away at the funeral. Everyone knows that.'

'Yes,' said Nan, 'but I forgot. I probably misheard or misunderstood.'

'Whatever you like, signora,' said Graziella dubiously.

'Don't talk about Graziella to anyone,' Nan warned Maria. 'Anyone at all. I don't want her in trouble when nothing really happened.'

'Something might have happened,' Maria suggested. She had been interrupted in mid-note.

'But it didn't.'

'Antonio says it's all over the village that Don Michele has run away.'

'Well, if he has, he's run away by himself,' said Nan.

Fortuno could hardly come to see Dickie now he was no longer ill. 'He never was ill,' Giuseppina told Antonio and they smiled at the implications. The Prescotts were together now all the time, apparently absorbed in each other. *He* is absorbed, thought Nan. Dickie ran in and out in the old way making noises. 'I'm a car,' he told Pina. '*Una macchina*.' He had learnt the word from Antonio. There was peace only when Molly Baghot took him off to the cherry tree or Nan let him carry scraps to the hens.

'They've booked another night,' Nan told Maria. 'The Peruzzis cancelled.'

'This is a beautiful spot,' Alan Prescott had said to her. 'And Claire hasn't seen Assisi, has she? Only would it be possible to leave Dickie here while we go sightseeing? It isn't much for a child, is it?'

So Dickie took the bowl of odds and ends for the hens and in the sudden calm Nan said to Giuseppina, 'Mr and Mrs Prescott are leaving about ten. Can you keep your eye on the little boy?' which gave Giuseppina an excuse for being slow at her work all morning and for ignoring Maria's periodic outbursts.

As the Prescotts left Fortuno arrived. 'May we talk in private?' he said to Nan. He could hear voices on the terrace. He walked into her sitting-room before she could speak.

'How very serious you are.' She opened the shutters a little. The sun spilled in across the stones. She saw the myriad motes of dust. All old houses are dusty, she thought; the dust of ages-old occupation, of generations coming and going. Cleaning only stirs it up, never banishes it entirely.

'Anna,' said Fortuno.

She turned slowly and found him still serious, frowning even. Has he brought bad news? she wondered.

'Don Michele is still missing.'

She felt a jolt, the clutch of fright. 'If he's run away he's run away by himself,' she had said to Maria, or something similar. She sensed Fortuno's extraordinary anxiety across the space between them, just as she had sensed Sister Angela's frustration through the crackling phone line. But why be anxious?

'He's a grown man,' she said lightly. 'He might look absurdly young but he's really grown up and quite sensible, more sensible than most young men of his age, probably, after years in a seminary and all the good advice Father Emilio hands out night and day. He might have needed to go off alone, to . . . to come to terms.'

'With whom?'

'With himself. Father Emilio told me he was resigned to giving up Graziella but . . . Who knows? He might still be struggling.'

'I think it's more serious.'

'That seems serious enough.'

'He's never been missing before.'

'He's never been in love before. At least, I don't suppose he has.'

'Father Emilio is worried.'

'I know that. He rang to tell me so.'

'Did you believe Don Michele's explanation for the cut on his head?'

Nan said nothing. She wondered what all this was

leading to and if, when whatever it was was reached, it would be the signal for another quarrel. I haven't the energy for a fight, she thought. She needed what little she felt she still had to parry Sister Angela's probing questions. I won't always be saved by a poor telephone line, she thought wryly.

'You know someone attacked him?'

'I think it was fairly obvious. D'you think it was a rival? Lots of the village boys covet Graziella.'

'There may be more to it than that.'

'Village troubles?' Villages were villages the world over, she thought, rife with evergreen resentment, ancient memories.

'You weren't here during the war. You don't know what it was like.'

'No,' said Nan. What else could she say?

'Did you know that his father was shot for betraying partisans?'

'Father Michele's? No, I didn't. Shot by whom?'

'Shot. It doesn't matter by whom.'

'I don't see what that has to do with Graziella, with his being in love, with his . . . disappearing.'

'Perhaps it has everything to do with it,' and Fortuno spread his fine hands in a sad gesture as if he were showing her the cloth of life with all its tight and intricate threads going this way and that but all connected, touching, leading one to another.

'You're being mysterious,' she accused. 'And melodramatic. What do you want to tell me?'

'If you know anything about all this, if Graziella has told you anything . . .'

'Why should she tell me anything?' said Nan evasively.

'Don Michele might be in danger.'

'How can he be? He's a priest. Everyone is co-operating to make sure he gets away with a whole skin. It's Graziella who's the only danger, isn't it? Next week she'll be in Perugia out of the way.' Her words fell over one another, were eccentric and unsuitable.

'Your Italian is abominable,' Fortuno told her.

Molly came up to dinner and played whist with Mrs Holland, Alan Prescott and Miss Elwes. 'I can't stand cards,' Claire Prescott said and went out on the terrace. Dickie got up twice for a drink and Maria said, 'The English send their children to bed too early,' and kept him in the kitchen until Nan came in to remonstrate. Fortuno rang to say that Father Michele was still missing and Graziella took the call and broke down, sobbing and shaking, in Nan's arms. Later, when Antonio took Molly and the girls down to the village, there was a 'to-do' as Maria called it. She had picked this up from Aunt Dot and it appealed to her, both the sound and the sense. 'Always with this girl there is a to-do,' she said to Nan. This time it was the case and the clothes. It was proving more difficult than expected to wear two of everything.

'I'll put the case in the cupboard with mine,' Nan said. 'We can deal with it another time. It won't be missed.'

It would, she knew. In a convent everything is accounted for: poverty, chastity and obedience see to it.

'I shall go to bed early,' she said to Maria when the car had gone.

'The Signora Prescott is in the garden,' Maria told her.

'There's a moon,' said Nan as if this explained such eccentricity.

'And Dr Fortuno?' asked Maria with an arch smile.

But Dr Fortuno arrived later, just when Nan, putting down her book thought: I should have gone to bed after all. I haven't taken in a word. She heard the car but thought it was Antonio returning, wondered idly if Maria had locked the front door and stretched . . .

'May I come in?' asked Fortuno.

He was in old trousers and a shirt. He looked a little dirty and untidy as if he had been crawling through undergrowth. She thought she saw a smear of blood.

'Yes, of course. Come in.'

He closed the door firmly. 'We've found him,' he said.

She felt a dreadful sinking, the instinct of disaster. Her heart sounded loud in her ears. 'Is he all right?'

'No. He's dead.'

She remembered the young man laid out on her kitchen table. His hair had been soft and unruly, his pale face just a boy's. Fortuno was saying softly, 'He was shot.'

'Murdered?'

'Yes, of course murdered. I warned you.'

'Did you?'

She felt astray in a strange country where she had never been before, as she had when finding Graziella sobbing by the roadside. It was as if . . . as if in the middle of an ordinary domestic drama she had stepped to the wings and found herself in another play on another stage – Euripides perhaps – and not knowing what lines to speak or even where to stand.

Since Fortuno said nothing and the silence stretched out she felt she must find something, anything to express her shock, her pity. But no words came. 'Your

Italian is abominable,' he had said. In English then.

In English all that came was: 'Thank God the nuns are there to comfort Graziella.'

12

THE new day was fine and clear. 'My last day,' said Mrs Holland at breakfast. 'I shall sit on the terrace.' Nan was serving. 'Why no Giuseppina?' asked Miss Elwes.

Guiseppina was in the kitchen, wan and distracted. 'Not fit to be seen,' said Maria. Graziella had not come to work. 'She's ill,' Guiseppina had said and had looked . . . frightened? There are things going on, Nan thought, that I know nothing about. And never shall. What was Graziella feeling? Did anyone at the convent care what she was feeling? Or did they consider that the young recovered quickly?

In the sunlight of this present the agony suffered in the long reaches of a distant night seemed unreal. Nan, recalling the astonishing pain interspersed with such astonishing numbness, and the dragged-out time, so slow that the clock hands scarcely moved, felt the stab of her own loss over again. How strange that it passes, she thought, bringing coffee to the Prescotts' table and smiling at Dickie who was making a valiant effort to sit up properly and eat tidily so as to avoid his father's wrath. In days or months or years it passes and finally one looks back down a long tunnel to something moving but inaudible, a shadow flickering, a faint impression. Only once, holding the baby in the bathroom, had she cried inwardly with the dizzying sense of bereavement returned in all its force: I want *my* baby. I want my baby.

'Madame Prunier is having breakfast in her room,' said Maria.

'But who took it up?'

'I did.' The sudden determined straightening of Maria's broad shoulders gave Nan to understand she could be relied on in a crisis.

Nan said, 'Pina hardly knows what she's doing.'

'The nuns were up all night. She says everyone was awake.'

'Why? Because of Don Michele?'

Maria was pretending indifference. 'Who knows? Probably that stupid girl kept them all up having hysteria.'

'Surely . . . even if they knew about Don Michele last night it wouldn't have been sensible to tell Graziella. She ought to have been asleep.'

'Word gets about,' said Maria.

When Nan rang the convent and asked for news a calm voice replied, 'I don't know how she is, signora. You must talk to Sister Angela.'

'Is Sister Angela available?'

'No, signora. She's at Mass.'

'I feel so helpless,' said Nan to Maria. 'And yet what on earth could I do?'

There was nothing she could do but keep the Villa

Giulia in order. All morning Giuseppina had a tendency to burst into tears and was slow and dropped things so that Nan harried her from room to room and made half the beds herself. At last, exasperated, she exclaimed, 'I don't see why *you* have to cry.'

'But he was so *gentile*, *simpatico*.'

So he was, thought Nan: kind, desperate to please. Had they after all been innocent lovers, lying together like children, touching but not possessing? She did not think so, yet it was easy to imagine that he had struggled before he gave in. He took things seriously, she thought. He always wanted to do what was right.

'Nature takes its course,' Maria said. 'Rain and sun and what do you get?'

'Weeds?' asked Nan.

'A glut. All these greens. How am I to use them up?'

The kitchen was hot and full of sun. 'I like light,' Maria had declared and refused to shut any out. She bore the heat without noticing it. 'It's like a Turkish bath,' Robin had declared and never ventured there. He was repelled by the atmosphere, charged with human endeavour: chopping, mashing, straining, stirring. Maria's great breasts heaved with sweat – the dark hairs above her sensuous mouth were beaded with it – and her fat feet in their old shoes slapped back and forth, back and forth. 'The kitchen's operatic,' Robin announced. The kitchen is life, thought Nan.

Now she was topping and tailing beans with a sort of fury. She ought to drive down to the village to make sure Molly Baghot was packed and ready to go. If I don't, she thought, no one else will, and then she'll lose the ticket, and run amok and . . .

'There's a policeman outside,' announced Giuseppina, coming in with a bundle of tablecloths and looking pale and frightened.

127

'Outside?'

'Did you want him inside, signora? A policeman?'

He was a perfectly unexceptional man, short, greying, tired. He spoke softly and succinctly and his questions went on and on, 'as if he hopes to wear me down', thought Nan. It was more likely he was simply being kind, thinking she might not understand him.

'You sent her on an errand. Where to? When was this?'

'She says she knew the Umbertis were away. You had forgotten. She thought she could have some time to herself. She was unhappy. She walked in the fields. How long was she missing?'

'Were you worried when she didn't return?'

'Do you think she arranged to meet Don Michele?'

'Sister Angela believes she meant to run away. Her clothes were missing. Now her clothes are back but her case has vanished. Are you sure she said nothing to you?'

'Signora, everyone's told me how you care for this girl. You didn't want her to go to Perugia. Did you suspect she and Don Michele might run off?'

As he said '*fuggire*' Nan suddenly saw them, the girl and the boy, running hand in hand through Concini's orchard.

'Signora, I'm sorry I have you ask so many questions.'

'So am I,' said Nan.

'What did he ask *you*?' to Maria among the vegetables.

'What time she left for Umberti's.'

'What did you say?'

'I said I didn't know. It was after siesta. You had sent her, I knew nothing.'

'And I said I didn't know anything.' Giuseppina reported.

I'm part of a conspiracy, thought Nan, appalled.

'It seems to me,' wrote Aunt Dot, 'that the best thing they could do would be to run away together. This would have the merit of creating a whole set of new problems. I've found,' and here Nan could imagine Aunt Dot's 'dry look' as she thought of it, 'this is often beneficial all round.'

I ran off with Robin, thought Nan.

It had not been like Graziella and Father Michele. It had been the rather abrupt culmination of an ordinary pedestrian courtship which had waited – 'underhand-edly' said Nan – on Evelyn's death. There would have been no marriage, she had often thought, if Evelyn had lived. It had not been a romance even, just a coming together of two lonely people and, with Evelyn desperately ill, the unhappiness and confusion that made marrying Robin seem sensible. But we did love each other, she thought.

'If in doubt, don't,' Aunt Dot had always preached. Even Aunt Dot, the only person Nan would certainly have invited, had missed the wedding. 'It all happened so quickly,' Nan wrote to her, ashamed now it was over. 'Robin said, "Let's get married tomorrow," so we did, and . . .' And Nan could only send a telegram to Aunt Dot.

'Had you any doubts?' was Aunt Dot's extraordinary response.

'No,' said Nan.

The doubts came afterwards.

'But afterwards you have to make the best of it,' said Aunt Dot.

*

Nan had rarely had to combat a guilty conscience and she grew short-tempered. After Giuseppina had been sick twice and sat about looking clammy and grey and desperate she snatched up the car keys and bundled her in. 'I don't know how we'll manage,' was Maria's parting shot.

'We'll manage,' said Nan.

At the convent they let her in with astonishment – and disapproval? She delivered Giuseppina into the hands of a squat plump motherly little novice.

'May I see Graziella?'

But Graziella was in bed. 'Not well, *poverina*,' whispered the nun. What a shock it had been, she admitted innocently, opening her eyes wide and crumpling the ends of her veil in soft fat hands.

'They must find whoever killed him,' said Nan and saw the hands fall still, twisted in the fine black cloth.

'No, signora. They'll never do that. This sort of thing has happened since the war ended.'

'The war ended a long time ago. In any case, it might have been someone who wanted him to stop seeing Graziella. A quarrel. An accident. Why should it be anything to do with the war?'

'It was not an accident, signora.'

'Signora Mortimer,' cried Sister Angela, gliding towards them rapidly. Her hands were folded under her scapular and her feet were invisible under the long skirts so that she appeared limbless. They never run, thought Nan, and they cast their eyes down ... modestly. Sister Angela reached her and she found herself staring into eyes of the palest blue which shone with 'holy fire'. 'Well, what else can it be?' Nan had asked Aunt Dot long ago.

'Signora Mortimer, a moment.'

'I'm sorry,' said Nan, backing away. 'I'm sorry, I don't have even a moment.'

'I ran away,' Nan confessed to Molly Baghot. They were sitting side by side on Molly's bed in Signora Falcone's best bedroom eating figs.

'Who wouldn't run away from that woman?' Molly asked. 'So certain of herself, so . . . fulfilled. Like Boadicea and the Head of Cheltenham Ladies' College in one. 'A flame of God' I read in a book about some martyr or other, one of those north country women they pressed and racked and practically tore limb from limb. That's who I think of when I see Sister Angela. Is it any wonder we ordinary mortals feel a little singed and run away?'

Nan said, 'You cheer me up.'

'I hope so. But no Graziella, no Pina . . . What will Maria do? Who will serve?'

'I'll serve. We'll manage. We've managed before.'

There was no sign, she thought anxiously, of imminent departure. Molly's silver brush and comb were still on the dressing-table, her slippers by the bed.

'I wondered if you'd like me to drive you to the station instead of getting a taxi.'

'The station? Oh, I'm not going to the station, dear.'

'But you said you had your ticket.'

'Now this has happened, how can I go? Poor Graziella. She confided in me. She said I was her friend.'

'You can't do anything for her, Molly.'

'I can be here. Then she'll know . . . If there's anything . . .'

'But the train. Mr Ruddock. Lily.'

'What has Lily to do with it?'

'Wasn't she going to meet you in Dover?'

Molly put up a tiny hand rather sticky with fig juice and touched Nan gently, almost pityingly, on the cheek. 'I wasn't going to Dover, dear. I was going to Rome.'

'Rome?' cried Nan.

Downstairs Signora Falcone repeated '*Si, Roma*,' and her eyes slid away, ashamed, and stared out of the open doorway into the street.

'I thought . . . I understood Mrs Baghot had bought her ticket to England.'

'She asked me to help her buy a ticket for Rome. She has never seen Rome, she said. She was going for two days. Only two days, signora.'

'Where was she going to stay?'

This question seriously puzzled Signora Falcone. Her eyes wandered back from the street and stretched in surprise. 'Why, a hotel, signora. A hotel, certainly.'

'Did she ask you to help her with that too?'

'No. Oh no. I thought that naturally she had arranged it with you, signora, since you're in the business.'

Nan's brow was puckered, her mouth folded tightly. 'It's not good for the skin. You'll look your age,' Aunt Dot would have warned. Signora Falcone only saw quite plainly that the Englishwoman was upset.

'Don't I know, signora,' she said comfortingly, putting a hand on Nan's arm. 'She's a difficult old lady.'

'I had to go straight away and send a telegram to Lily,' Nan said to Maria.

In the house the silence was profound and unusual. Nan nearly asked, 'Where is everybody?' before she remembered. Maria told her that Dr Fortuno was in the garden and was disconsolate.

'Are you here as a friend or a medical man?' Nan

asked him. He was sitting on the stone seat at the end of the weedy gravel walk.

Fortuno considered her, discerned the lines of strain, naturally misinterpreted them and said humbly, 'A friend of course. If I insulted you I'm sorry.'

'You only spoke the truth.'

'In general,' he conceded, trying to make amends, 'you speak Italian well.'

'The thing is,' and Nan plucked at the rose leaning over the wall which showered petals over them both, 'the thing is I can't cope with philosophy, politics and moral argument. My speciality is menus.'

He looked bewildered. 'Menus?'

'Never mind. Is there anything in particular? Have you come to catch a last glimpse of Claire Prescott?'

'You're very aggressive this morning.'

'I'm very busy this morning.'

'I've been to see Graziella. I had to give her an injection, a sedative. She was wild, screaming and screaming. She wanted to see his body.'

'I can understand that.'

'The police have it. There's nothing much I can do there. And the nuns tell her it's morbid.'

The rose petals were silky in her palm. They smelled of cloves, she thought, surprised, lifting them to her nose.

'Where was he found? Nobody told me.'

'Up on the hill. By the old tower.'

'Why up there? Why would he go up there?'

Fortuno shrugged. 'It's quiet. There are no houses. This,' and he nodded at the Villa Giulia shaded by its trees and rosemary and climbing roses, 'is the nearest.'

There's the view, she thought suddenly, the view all my guests walk up there for: the oaks, the green folds of the valleys, the patterns of cultivated land, the hilltop villages, the high pastures of sheep and cattle. Mrs Holland has eaten her picnic on the warm stones of the ruined watch tower. Miss Elwes has sketched there for hours. Robin and I used to stand there and think how beautiful . . .

'There shouldn't be any death in a place like that,' she said stupidly.

'Oh, it's an old execution ground,' he replied easily, as if such a thing were too ordinary to be shocking.

'Whose execution ground?'

'Who can say? Perhaps before the Romans came the tribes were using it. It goes back, far back.'

'It wasn't the tribes who killed Don Michele.'

'Now and again this sort of thing happens.'

'He was too young to have fought in the war. Besides, he was a priest.'

'Not too young to have been a messenger.'

'Too young to know what it was all about.' Nan pulled down another spray of roses and crumbled the dead heads briskly. 'Do you think he was killed by whoever hit him in my meadow?'

'It's possible.'

'Did anyone tell the police about that?'

'I doubt it.'

'Shouldn't we?'

'There's no point, Anna.'

'But . . .'

'There's no point. And there'll never be any proof. The gun which fired that bullet will never be found.'

Nan let go of the roses and they swayed above her, transparent as white muslin. 'Isn't it a mortal sin to kill a priest?'

Fortuno smiled sadly. 'Murder is a mortal sin.'

The petals were all around them. Nan brushed one from her blouse. She must go in. She must help Maria. She must drive out to the Andreottos to see if Luisella would care to help at dinner . . .

'Do you know who it was?' she whispered.

'No.'

She looked into his face and saw it was the truth. He repeated: 'No, Anna. I don't know.'

She began to walk back to the house, feeling as if she had great weights on her legs. And on my heart, she thought.

13

FATHER Michele was buried quietly. 'Without anyone knowing,' said Nan bitterly. 'He's been tidied away. Like Graziella.' For the convent's doors could close almost as surely as those of the grave.

'There was no one there,' reported Pina. 'Only an old uncle and Father Emilio.'

'But who carried the coffin?' asked Nan.

'Coffin-bearers,' said Pina. 'Who else?' They had been men from the uncle's village, a little arrangement of Father Emilio's to avoid embarrassment. There was no point in telling this to the Signora, though. These days she took such things to heart and flew into passions. 'What passion!' Pina had grown used to remarking to Maria, amazed and delighted. But there were some things best left alone.

'Poor Father Michele,' said Nan. She had liked him. He had been so earnest and had made her feel tender, amused.

'Poor young fool,' snapped Maria, who was making

pasta. Her hands slapped back and forth, back and forth, and there was a sudden fine mist of flour rising.

And that, thought Nan, was Cittavigile's epitaph for a murdered man.

Nan was troubled. The furious way she battled through the day showed only the depth of her trouble, not its cause. It was something to do, she thought, with Italy and her life in Italy, her years of hoping, striving, to belong. Besides this she felt as if she had lost her grip on time as well as place. She had to ask Maria what year it was when she wrote a cheque. 'It's understandable,' said Maria in a melancholy voice. 'This part of the world is so behind the rest it might as well be fourteen hundred, fifteen hundred ... If we had a washing machine, signora, how much better it would be.'

'I never thought I'd have a daughter like that,' Evelyn had once said to Aunt Dot while drinking tea in the garden in Cambridge. It had been a pleasant garden, very much of its time, fragrant with lupins and cascading rockery plants.

'Like what?'

'Vague. Clumsy. An odd child.'

'She seems quite normal to me.'

If I had a child, thought Aunt Dot, I would overlook every fault, but perhaps after all parenthood was not what she supposed. She longed for a child with the strenuous longing no power in life can assuage, though the passing years appear to make such desires irrelevant. 'Perhaps you should encourage her more,' she suggested. You have such a dampening effect, she might have added.

'Encourage her in what?'

'In everything. In life.'

'What rubbish you talk sometimes.'

Dot stared across the lawn to where Nan was cutting dead heads off the roses. There was a droop to her shoulders, that quick anxious glancing round as if, before her mother spoke, she might perceive what it was she had done wrong. She'll never get it right, thought Dot sadly, because it's not what she does but what she is that Evelyn objects to, poor kid.

'She's nearly fifteen,' said Evelyn, 'and so dreadfully . . . sturdy.'

'Plump. She'll grow out of it.'

'And she's not clever. "Satisfactory" they tell me.'

'What sort of child did you want, for God's sake?'

'I never really got on with your mother,' Aunt Dot told Nan years later.

'Very few people did,' said Nan with feeling.

When the prison door had opened she had stepped through only to find the free air frightening. She had felt like this as a child running home across Coe Fen, felt abandoned to the coming dark, that moment on the edge of night when old fears and primitive memory rise up and make the flesh creep. How she had run! She had run in through the gate and seen with bursting relief that the lights were on, the rooms were ordinary, homely, warm. Like that child she had ducked and run towards the warm ordinary room Robin had prepared for her and the door had closed tight behind her.

'Another prison,' said Aunt Dot, spring-cleaning Laburnum Lodge with old Ivy – 'Two stiff old maids,' she wrote to Nan – taking the carpet-beater to the worn Victorian runners and the threadbare mats.

Even the Villa Giulia had been made safe and normal with Robin. When Nan had said, 'I wouldn't know how to live in such a place,' he had said bluntly, 'You simply live in it,' without knowing what she meant. 'It will run itself,' he had assured her, or: 'Maria will see to it,' and had made her walk to the top of the hill to look at the view. 'We could look at the view from the meadow,' Nan had said, 'and I'd still have time to ask Maria about that recipe for peppers.'

Another time: 'We still behave like tourists though we've been here a year,' she told him.

'Does it matter? In a way we are tourists.'

'We're not. We're residents. We live here. How can we expect them to take us seriously if we never go anywhere without a guidebook?'

'Darling, they're only people like us. They understand.'

'I don't think they are like us.'

At last, exasperated: 'It really doesn't matter, does it,' Robin said, 'what they think?'

'It ought to,' said Nan.

'Signora, what about the Americans?' asked Maria.

'What Americans?' Nan had hardly got over the shock of Claire Prescott crying into her shoulder, Dickie howling, Antonio forgetting a last case on the steps . . .

'Signora, signora,' and Maria threw up her hands in horror. I wish I could do that convincingly, thought Nan. 'From Massa Chuse Setts.'

'Oh!' cried Nan. 'Mr and Mrs Greenway. Oh, my God!'

'I'm afraid we're short-handed,' she told the Greenways before dinner, taking them drinks on the terrace.

They nodded sympathetically, not believing her. They were rather quiet because they were mutually astonished: at Nan, at the house, at Italy.

'I'm sure it's not what we're used to and that's a fact,' Greenway said softly as Nan retreated. He gazed after her slender back and bronze hair. And the house. 'Shabby,' he said. The paint was peeling, there were rose petals all over the front steps, there were weeds. The sanitaryware in his bathroom was old. 'It's marble,' said his wife. 'And there's hot water, dear. Try.'

'We usually stay in big hotels,' he confided to Molly Baghot.

'How sad for you,' said Molly.

Dinner too was a revelation. Maria, single-handed, had produced a meal worthy of the Palazzo Andreone. 'Really too extravagant,' said Nan, who would have to pay the bills.

'Food strengthens the heart,' said Maria.

When the telephone rang it was Fortuno. 'Are you busy?'

'A little.'

'I think you should see Graziella.'

'I could drive down. I have to serve the coffee first.'

'I'll come up for you. Half an hour.'

Maria set out the coffee cups with trembling hands. 'She is dying then,' she said.

'How could she be dying? Anyway, what is it to you? You called her a whore.'

'Still . . . Holy Mary, I wouldn't wish her dead.'

Nan went for a jacket. 'I'm afraid I have to go out and the nights are often chilly,' she told the Greenways, who were in the hall. They were by now quite fuddled with strangeness and inclined to be silent. Maria's splendid meal, so unlike anything they had ever eaten, had filled them up but cast them down, down to where prickling anxieties about so much foreignness cast unavoidable gloom. They looked at Nan and saw a woman

of poise and purpose running downstairs in a soft knitted jacket the colour of bilberries. 'Pretty,' said Mrs
Greenway. They had understood that she was English
but she did not look English, though she was pale with
faint freckles and had, they supposed, the right kind of
accent. She could have been anything: French, Italian,
anything. She called 'Goodnight' and gave them a
charming, distracted smile and ran out into the cool resin-
scented night to where the car waited by the steps.

'She says she wants to die,' Fortuno said as they ground
between the gates and turned left into the road. 'She
weeps and screams.' He spoke English. Nan wondered
if he felt the language was better suited to such a crisis.
'Sister Angela can do nothing with her,' he continued.
'Nor can I. And now . . . They asked me to fetch you.'

'What can I do?'

'Somebody has to calm her. She says you were good
to her, you and Mrs Baghot.'

The cypresses fled away into the night. They were
coming to the village.

'You're very worried,' Nan said. She had seldom
seen him worried but now it occurred to her it was
because she had never noticed such things. 'I was too
self-centred,' she said afterwards to Aunt Dot.

'She might do herself harm.'

'I thought you'd given her an injection?'

'I can't go on giving injections.'

'I suppose not.'

They had left the village behind. In a moment the
convent walls would come in sight. What had it cost
Sister Angela to ask for the Englishwoman from the
Villa Giulia? 'She scares me silly,' Nan had once told
Robin. 'She's shorter than you,' Robin had said, as if

height gave power. In some people, Nan wanted to tell him, life burns twice as brightly tempering an implacable will. What she wanted she would get, from the community, from the village, from the Bishop if local rumour were true. From God? I last prayed in that dreadful hospital in London, she thought, and nobody answered, not even Robin answered. He told me everything was all right; I was safe; there would be other babies.

The great lock in the outer gate, inadequately oiled since the sixteenth century, was slow to turn. The bolts made a great iron clanging in the quiet. Nan and Fortuno crossed the courtyard side by side, silent, and stepped into an echo of holy chant and the sweetness of incense. This time the door into the orphanage was open and here the corridors were terracotta tile and white paint.

'Thank you for coming,' said Sister Angela, holding out a hand.

They climbed stairs. Nan, gazing about, felt lost. The lights on the wall were very dim, the corridor here a mirror image of the one below except that now the doors were flanked by little plaster saints in niches, so that one might say that one had slept in St Anthony's or St Ursula's or St Peter's.

'How is she now?' Fortuno asked. He was subdued, Nan saw. But all men seemed subdued here, she remembered.

'Much the same.'

'Then I'll wait here.'

He and Sister Perpetua remained in the corridor. Sister Angela led Nan a little further.

'Do you want me to come in?'

'No,' said Nan in a whisper. To what was she being ushered with such gentle consideration? 'No, I'll be all right.'

142

'Go in then,' Sister Angela told her and swung open the door just enough for her to pass through.

'Graziella?'

It was a small single room like a cell. A nun's room? There was a crucifix on the wall. The light was poor. In the bed was a humped figure making inhuman noises.

'Graziella,' and Nan put a hand to the damp straggling hair.

'Signora Mortimer.' The figure moved, turned over, a wretched hot exhausted thing, scarcely recognizable.

Nan sat on the edge of the narrow bed and smoothed back the black hair. The girl's eyes were so lost in the puffy red flesh that she could not read their expression, and her skin was mottled and raw and shiny. She shook all the time. Even when Nan held her, soothing her like a baby, she still shook and seemed to strain this way and that.

'I want to die,' came the cracked old-woman voice.

'Yes, I know.'

'I couldn't save him.'

'Keep still,' said Nan. 'Don't cry any more.'

'I knew . . . I knew . . .'

'Hush,' said Nan. She bent to kiss the head cradled between her breasts and closed her eyes, to shut out what Graziella knew, to shut out the spartan room, the sight of such distress, the feeble lamp casting its tragic pallor. But in the dark behind her eyelids she saw again the road from Cittavigile, the figure stumbling in the light from the car, the girl's hair wrapped round them both in the cool blustering air. She heard again her own voice: Why were you on this road? Nowhere near Concini's. Nowhere near . . . Why . . . Why?

*

Fortuno stopped the car under the cypresses. He rolled down the window and lit a cigarette.

'What did you say to calm her?'

'Nothing really.'

'Sister Angela was hoping for a miracle and now she has one.'

'Only that the poor girl's gone to sleep.'

'Properly, peacefully to sleep.'

'It was bound to happen sooner or later,' said the cold, hard, distant Nan who had emerged from that little cell in the convent.

There was a silence. He can't think what to say, thought Nan, but she was too tired to be surprised, too tired to speak herself. Then he stirred abruptly, drawing on the cigarette.

'You shouldn't have interfered.'

'Interfered?'

'You spoke up for them, encouraged them.'

'I never *encouraged* them. I simply . . .'

'Old Mrs Baghot too. It was . . . misguided.' He shook ash out of the window.

'I didn't do anything,' protested Nan, stung by the injustice. 'I only beat my hands against a wall. Father Emilio, Sister Angela, even you . . . A wall,' said Nan, remembering all that indignation spilled for nothing.

'There was a lot of fuss.'

'So there should have been.'

'If they'd been separated quietly, if things had returned to normal, there would have been no need . . .'

'To kill him?' asked Nan.

'Old jealousies, new . . . Loyalty, honour, family . . . How could you understand? It was,' and his hands described it, so that she saw the vat, the rising skins, the bubbles. 'It was a ferment,' he said. He tried the word again; he was unsure of it. At any other time he would have asked her, 'Is that right? Ferment?' Now he looked steadfastly through the windscreen, his elbow lodged in the open window, the cigarette held loosely between his fingers. 'Anna, you shouldn't have interfered. The whole village knew about it, how you felt . . .'

'No one knew how I felt. I did what I thought was right.'

'By taking sides with a girl of sixteen and a priest?'

'Or simply with two young people in love.'

'There was nothing simple about it. There was so much . . . You had no idea . . .'

'Then why didn't someone explain?'

'It was old unfinished business. Cittavigile business.'

'Which, of course, is nothing to do with outsiders.'

Her heart ached. Instinctively she leaned forward as if easing real pain. She closed her eyes. She saw Father Michele, who should have been a missionary, cycling through the bush to spread the Word. Then she saw Graziella sobbing, face and fingers driven into the pillow, overcome by grief, by guilt. 'I knew . . . I knew . . .' she had cried. Had she told them about Concini's, known they would come there? Had they taken her with them up the hill, held her to watch him die? No, no, no, pleaded Nan silently.

'Take me home,' she commanded, opening her eyes.

She did not speak again. When he drew up by the steps she went in without looking back, closing the door on him – and on Cittavigile, she thought. In the hall Maria was waiting up. She was in a dressing-gown and her hair flowed down over her massive shoulders. She took one look at Nan's face and held out her arms.

'*Cara*,' she said.

14

IN spite of everything, life goes on, thought Nan. She thought it might be a sign of age that time seemed more relentless in its passing so that one scarcely grappled with one problem before it was yesterday's concern and today ... Today it's something else, she told herself. Still, murder, war, revolution, the beans must be picked.

'She's doing my job,' complained Antonio to Maria, but Maria shushed him impatiently and went on with her chopping. 'Let her. Let her do what she likes.'

The beans were fugitive, hiding amid heavy foliage. Nan worked along the row growing hot. She had expected such a simple job to calm her, keep hands and mind occupied, but her hands brushed back and forth through the harsh leaves automatically and her mind 'flew off', she said to herself. There was a pattern, if only she could see it, the pattern in the cloth of life Fortuno had spread for her. Like something glimpsed from the corner of the eye the strands wove in and out, in and out. I am one of those strands, she thought, and the beans fell more and more slowly. I stayed on after Robin died when they all thought I would leave; I kept Molly Baghot here when she should have gone home to Lily. Because of me, because of Molly, there was a fuss over Graziella. *Una scenata*. But what was it we stirred up between us? Old bitterness, new bitterness, old and new revenges . . . violence.

Nan shivered, and her hands were still, her head bowed over the basket.

'Signora, *per favore*,' said Antonio, taking the basket from her.

'I haven't finished.'

'You look unwell, signora. Go in. Lie down. Maria will bring you wine.' He held on to the basket with proprietorial firmness.

Nan went in but was back almost immediately with a bucket of kitchen scraps for the hens, another of Antonio's jobs. But they're my hens, it's my bucket, she reminded herself childishly. She was still trying to separate the threads of life. Things go on because they have to, she thought; there are always mouths to feed, weeds to pull, floors to sweep. 'What a pity there aren't any children,' people had said after Robin died, but the Villa Giulia was as exacting as any child, dragging her back from the luxury of self-indulgent grief. 'I ought to go back to England,' she had said to Degnare. 'Why?' he asked. 'All I have is here,' she said to Aunt Dot which was not true because she had Laburnum Lodge. 'The truth is I would rather have the Villa Giulia,' said Nan. She thought it was because Robin had found it and suggested they live there, because Robin had died in it: 'As if dying in a house hallows it in some way,' Nan said afterwards, 'which is ridiculous. We all have to die somewhere.' All that summer she was in a daze, a daze of grief and love. She thought she was loving the villa for Robin's sake but deep down she knew it was for its own. My bones knew it, she thought. She did not want her mind to acknowledge it: it seemed disloyal to Robin.

'The best house in the district,' Degnare pointed out. 'What gardens! What views!'

'The gardens have gone to ruin,' Nan said.

'But the views . . .'

No, the views haven't gone to ruin, she thought. Not yet. The war has left them untouched. They may remain untouched for fifty, a hundred years to come. Only some farms are empty, some houses in the high villages, because the young men are going to work in the factories in the north.

'If you stay, Maria will keep her job,' Degnare had wheedled. 'And Antonio. And Pia.'

'I can't afford them,' she had insisted. It was then that he had suggested the hotel.

'A cook is such a luxury,' she had said to Robin in the beginning.

'We deserve one luxury surely?' he had replied.

Later: 'I can't do without Maria,' she had said. By then Robin knew he was dying. I suppose he always knew he was dying, thought Nan, and I was too stupid and childish and self-involved to know it too.

The hens picked over the scraps and complained at the selection. Nan went in again. In the hall the telephone was shrilling among a storm of petals.

'Pina!' cried Nan as she picked it up.

'*Pronto*,' said an English voice.

'Aunt Dot?'

'Your last letter sent me for my suitcase. I'm in Dover. It's pouring with rain. I'll be with you shortly.'

'Shortly?' Nan was astounded.

'Well, there's all France in front,' Aunt Dot conceded. 'And half Italy.'

When Nan went to the kitchen to announce the news Maria said, 'Praise the saints,' and crossed herself, something Nan had never seen her do before.

'But signora,' said Pina, hurrying in with the rose petals scooped in a duster. 'Where can we put her to sleep? The house is full.'

'So it is,' said Nan. So that is tomorrow's crisis, she was thinking, and she saw the threads of Fate woven in and out, drawing tighter and tighter.

'There's no point in worrying before it happens,' Maria threw over her shoulder as she carried on, to the larders, to the table, to the stove.

'Before what happens?' Giuseppina asked, looking anxious.

'Anything,' said Maria.

'You must have bribed the engine drivers,' Nan said, savouring the gin.

They were on the terrace and alone. It was not even lunch-time. Yet here I am with my feet up and a gin in my hand, thought Nan.

'I felt I had to come,' Aunt Dot confessed, 'when I detected a hysterical note in your letters. It didn't sound like you.'

'I feel turned inside out. Is that foolish?'

'Not if that's what you feel.'

'Ever since the Major died I've been ... I don't know, knocked off course.'

Or made to take notice again, thought Aunt Dot. 'I could tell, dear. But you didn't seem to be taking it calmly. What about my Dr Fortuno in love?'

'He wasn't in love, only . . .'

'There you are. Such disapproval.'

'But it was in my house, under the husband's nose.'

'Perhaps the husband should have looked underneath his nose a little sooner,' remarked Aunt Dot. She re-settled her straw hat – high-crowned, small-brimmed – and gazed with amusement at Nan's face, tipped up so that she could see the sky between the vine leaves. 'There are rose petals everywhere.'

'Pina can't concentrate. She forgets. And she doesn't get on with Pia.'

'Old Pia?'

'Oh, I drove down to the village and fell on my knees yesterday and she came back.'

'You see,' said Aunt Dot, 'how people rise to the occasion.'

'Only out of curiosity,' said Nan.

It was becoming imperative to deliver Molly Baghot to the waiting Lily before, as Nan predicted, she ran amok. She had already been over to the bakery, rising in the small hours and pattering out in her nightdress to see what they were doing. She was amusing and they made her welcome but she poked her fingers into the dough and asked too many questions, and though it was obvious she meant well she was like a mischievous child; and like a mischievous child she was escorted back to Signora Falcone's. 'But what can I do about it?' asked Nan.

Degnare said, 'I've had two telegrams asking where she is.'

She was walking the hills, plaguing the bakery, re-arranging Signora Falcone's ornaments, arguing with Father Emilio. In passing she said to Aunt Dot, 'I've never been happier,' and flitted away to the meadow with a sketchbook, 'Though I can't really draw at all,' she said.

Signora Falcone was stout and short of breath. Her complaint to Dr Fortuno was delivered in a harsh affecting voice while one hand clutched the breast over her suffering heart.

'Two days. Two days, the signora said. And now it's a week, soon two. And then what? Of course there's the money, but money . . .' and she shrugged, speechless, as if it was impossible to say how little money meant in such circumstances.

'Mrs Baghot has outstayed her welcome,' Dr Fortuno told Aunt Dot. He had come upon her gardening, attacking the hedges and the paths at the same time, dropping shears to pluck up the hoe and then the hoe to snatch at the shears.

'I'll be finished along here by lunch,' she said with satisfaction.

'It's a remarkable improvement. But you ought to sit a while on the terrace, and have some lemonade.'

'Lemonade?' cried Aunt Dot and her eyebrows rose to meet her hat brim.

'Mrs Baghot . . .' he pursued, taken aback.

'I'll mention it to Nan but I don't see what she can do. Molly Baghot isn't her responsibility. If the poor woman doesn't want to go how can we make her?'

'Signora Mortimer is paying Mrs Baghot's bills.'

Aunt Dot brushed the hedgecuttings to the ground and raked them up briskly along with the weeds. 'Do you suggest she leaves the woman destitute?'

'How else can she be persuaded to go home?'

'I don't think she looks on England as home.'

'Her sister . . .'

'Sisters, mothers, daughters,' exclaimed Aunt Dot. 'We don't all fall on each other's necks in a passion of affection. Have you a light?' She had rested the hoe and rake together against her hip and had shaken a packet of cigarettes from the pocket of her skirt.

'She's a tiresome old lady,' he said, bending with his hand cupped about the flame.

Aunt Dot threw down the rake and plied the hoe violently in the greenery about his feet. He stepped back, alarmed.

'There ought to be more tiresome old ladies,' she said. 'It might ginger things up.'

'He made me cross,' Aunt Dot told Nan later.

'But things are already gingered up. Too much. There's been a murder, remember?'

They were driving to the convent and the Morris was backfiring. They made an explosive entrance to Citta-vigile and it was a relief after that to turn off the engine and get out and hang on the solemn bell, listening for the quiet measured tread of a nun's shoes and the drawing-back of the bolts.

'It's like a fortress,' said Aunt Dot.

They walked in 'like two schoolgirls in a crocodile', thought Nan. The long empty corridors discouraged talk. When they emerged through a low door into the cloister garden the heat and sunlight seemed overpowering. Graziella sat on a stone bench with embroidery in her lap.

'How are you?' Nan began the ritual. The embroidery, she saw, was in reality just darning: a smock, and under it a small shirt, and on the ground a basket of socks.

'I'm all right. How are you, signora?'

The beautiful young face looked old, Nan thought: calm, recovered, old. The eyes were no longer reddened but they held no light. The pliable young hands, though they moved and worked, pushing the needle in and out, seemed lifeless.

'I'm going to Perugia tomorrow,' the girl said. 'I'll be glad to go.'

'They've killed the child,' declared Aunt Dot, opening the car door and hurrying to get in.

The weather was capricious for a few days. There were disgruntled guests and the flurry of borrowed raincoats. The Greenways, who were not enjoying themselves, asked Nan mournfully, 'Should it be like this?' for they had imagined Italy eternally scalded by the blessed sun.

'Well, there are mountains,' Nan pointed out.

'Rain is good for the vegetables,' said Antonio, who met them in the garden. They did not understand him but nodded pleasantly, rushing away as more drops began to fall.

Molly acquired a large black umbrella – 'episcopal' said Aunt Dot – and continued to irritate Cittavigile, while at the Villa Giulia the telephone rang frequently with enquiries from England. 'You must come here yourself and fetch her,' was Nan's final exasperated proposal.

So next it was: 'Miss Trewarden arriving Rome Tuesday.'

'What am I supposed to do about it?' demanded Nan, holding the telegram under Aunt Dot's nose.

'Perhaps they expect you to meet her.'

'In Rome?'

'Is it very far?'

'Miles. In any case, why should I?'

Aunt Dot had recourse to a map of Italy and found out just how far Rome was from the Villa Giulia on its remote hill.

'Oh, this is such an isolated house!' Maria said.

'Especially to someone who's lived in Venice,' said Aunt Dot kindly.

'*Venezia!*' shrieked Maria. 'Too much water. All water, signora. Damp, smells, water, water . . .'

Aunt Dot escaped to the terrace and found Father Emilio hesitating under the dripping vine.

'You ought to come in,' she told him, 'before you get rheumatism. Nobody should ever sit in wet chairs.'

'Signora Mortimer . . .' he began. He had not understood a word.

'Oh, Nan won't mind . . .'

'Signora Mortimer and I have quarrelled.'

'. . . if you wipe your feet.'

Over wine and Maria's almond biscuits he ceased to look humble and expressed his opinion on what to do with the Signora Baggotta.

'That's Graziella's name for her,' Nan said softly and an awkward silence fell.

'The girl is safe in Perugia,' he said heavily.

'Safe?' said Nan. You've won, said her expression. You knew all along you'd win. He met her accusing eyes briefly and turned back to the biscuits.

'Signora Baghot,' and he made an effort. 'Signora Baghot must be persuaded to catch a train.'

'Oh,' cried Nan sharply, 'how glad I'll be when you've persuaded her. It needs someone like you to do it, someone with authority.'

So later when Signora Falcone asked if Father Emilio could 'do something' about the old woman he replied sadly that he had no influence at the Villa Giulia and he doubted he had much with Molly herself. He spread out his hands as if to demonstrate the unpredictability of women.

'Father Emilio gives me a sermon a day,' Molly told Maria. '*Un sermone ogni giorno.* Of course, I don't know what he's saying but I try to look interested.'

'At bottom,' said Maria, 'he is a good man.'

He had been sent a replacement for Father Michele in the shape of a bouncing young man from Pisa who had his heart set already on purple socks and a desk job in the Vatican. 'He must be disappointed in Cittavigile then,' said Nan, feeling a pang for Father Michele. A motherly pang, she thought. But I never had a son, I had a daughter.

'Pisa,' said Aunt Dot. 'Is a priest from Pisa acceptable?'

'Father Michele was local and look what happened.'

'Yes,' agreed Maria. 'Better a stranger even if he does talk through his nose.'

Trying to help his superior and no doubt with every good intention, Father Pietro talked through his nose at Molly Baghot and made her indignant. 'He lectures me,' she told Nan, though about what she was unclear. In consequence she spent more time at the Villa Giulia. 'Avoiding the clergy,' commented Aunt Dot.

Domestic crises dissolve sympathy in proportion. 'In proportion to what?' asked Aunt Dot. 'In proportion to the number of crises,' replied Nan. The whole world was at war: Molly with the village, Giuseppina with Pia, Aunt Dot with Dr Fortuno, Maria with almost everyone . . . And on top another telegram: 'Train arriving Rome 10.30. Please advise transport Villa Giulia.'

'I suppose there are local trains,' said Aunt Dot

dubiously and into her head came lines from 'Adlestrop' which she felt, with a few amendments, might be successfully applied to Italian country stations.

'They don't come up here,' said Nan. 'If she has to come to Rome she'll have to hire a car or get a taxi.'

Her temper was not improved since the day she had driven down to the convent to say goodbye to Graziella and give her, a little ashamed, the few gifts she had been able to muster in the time: a new slip, a record, a box of English chocolates. The girl had been sitting in the garden again, and again with the basket of mending at her feet. 'Only she wasn't mending,' Nan reported to Aunt Dot. 'She was crying.'

'My fingers are so sore,' Graziella had said, turning them over for inspection. 'I hate sewing.' As she spoke the tears ran silently from her eyes, ran and ran. It was as if some natural check had been suspended; as if, in time, she must dissolve away.

Nan offered the presents. 'But keep them in the bag. Sister Angela might not approve.' As if, she thought, any strange bag brought into this place might escape thorough investigation. Conspirators, they bent close. 'You're so kind,' said Graziella, 'you and the Signora Baggotta,' and she brought out Molly's gift from beneath the handkerchiefs and pinafores: a tortoiseshell brush, comb and mirror. 'For my dressing-table,' she said, though there were no dressing-tables, Nan suspected, in the convent in Perugia, but only a utilitarian chest of drawers under the crucifix. Then: 'Where did Molly get them?' asked the inner voice. 'Assisi? Gubbio?' Such things were not for sale in Cittavigile. And it was my money, thought Nan.

'*Buon giorno*,' said the voice of Dr Fortuno.

'As the personification of guilt you could hardly have

been surpassed,' he said afterwards, escorting Nan to the gate.

'You crept up on us.'

'Sister Angela wanted to know what was in the bag.'

'She could have come out herself and asked.'

'She cares for the girls, you know. She worries for them. She's not the ogre you like to think her. It's a heavy responsibility.'

'But what did she think I had in the bag? Heretical literature? Black lace underwear?'

He laughed, but it was a guarded laugh. He was not sure of her. She had grown unpredictable, inclined to flash out, to throw his words in his teeth, to mock.

'Anna . . .'

'Don't call me that,' she cried, the last thing he had been expecting. 'My name's Annette. And I'm Nan to my friends, Nan to everyone.'

While he grappled with the last door she was away across the courtyard, and as he emerged from the gate he heard the uneven growl of the Morris's engine and the grinding of wheels over stones.

So when he next met her, at Molly's bedside, he was careful to treat her with impeccable formality, as if they were strangers.

Which we are, thought Nan sadly.

15

Because the early mornings at the Villa Giulia were always so beautiful Nan was usually in the garden by six. The world was fresh then: there was the smell of damp and green and the roses on the weathered old walls were tight in bud or only half-open. This morning she sat on the stone seat to write a letter to Graziella and she sat and sat, the pad aslant on her knee, the sun climbing, not a word on the paper. 'I hope you will be happy,' she managed at last but then crumpled it and dropped it at her feet. 'I hope you'll like Perugia,' was her next attempt.

As she looked down the path Aunt Dot had so furiously weeded and trimmed, Nan could remember Robin saying, 'If we could afford another gardener . . .'

'We can barely afford one,' she had pointed out.

'I suppose Antonio couldn't . . .'

'Antonio only does vegetables.'

'Surely he could cut a hedge?'

'It's not a question of being able to, it's a question of being willing.'

Antonio helped start the Morris; he mended the chicken run, the gateposts, the kitchen plumbing. He was fond of saying, 'I did this . . . or that . . . for the other signora,' meaning the previous owner of the Villa Giulia. In the beginning Nan naively believed he had accepted her, that he was just being kind in telling her how it had always been done. But Maria said ominously, 'He doesn't want to give up his bad habits. If you argue with him, he'll become a mule.'

He was a mule already. 'The other signora told me it must always be like this,' he would say, or: 'The other signora said it mustn't be touched in November – it would die.' 'I'm tired of the other signora,' said Nan but she could not get him to do what she wanted unless it was something the other signora had sanctioned. She realized how poorly she measured up. 'How kind she was,' said Antonio. 'How beautiful, how well-bred.' His hands described her in the air, a woman of irrepressible virtue. 'And I'm none of those things,' said Nan. She ceased sending messages to the vegetable garden.

'When is he to pick the lettuces?' asked Maria.

'When he feels like it,' Nan said.

'Do you want lots of courgettes, signora, or only a few?' asked Maria.

'Whatever Antonio thinks best.'

To Robin Nan said, 'I'm no good at being in charge. Why didn't you marry a sensible competent sort of wife who could keep servants in order? Like Aunt Dot.'

'Aunt Dot's really no more domesticated than you are,' Robin told her after considering the matter.

'But she knows how to get her own way.'

Nan grew so tired of being compared with the previous signora that she stayed away from the kitchen, greeted

Antonio with perfunctory politeness and passed over his wages in silence.

'The signora is offended,' he said to Maria.

'What did you expect?'

He did not like to think she was angry. He might be told to leave. Besides, she was young and good-looking and she meant to do what was right. Her only fault was that she was English. 'But she can't help that,' he said magnanimously.

He sent a peace-offering of the tenderest young vegetables arranged artistically in a great flat basket.

'They're our vegetables,' Robin reminded her when she had run to him in a little flurry of happiness and relief. 'He only had to pick them.'

'It must have taken him hours.'

'Then why couldn't he have done whatever you asked without a fuss? That would only have taken minutes.'

'But . . .' began Nan.

Though she had cursed the man yesterday and might again tomorrow she could appreciate his gesture, the vegetable still-life. She saw its significance. 'You let your emotions run away,' grumbled Robin. 'You're too soft. Anyone would think he'd put himself out for you.'

'But he has in his own way.'

'He'll know he can get away with anything now.'

Nan thought: I'm too emotional for Robin but not emotional enough for Maria.

In the garden, writing her letter to Graziella, the new sun warming her cheek, she could hear Antonio whistling on the other side of the wall.

'No, signora,' he had said outright when she had asked if he might trim the hedges and keep down the weeds after Robin died, but she had noticed a general air of tidying up as if, early or late but unobserved, he had passed by. He mowed the meadow with a scythe and his vegetables were cosseted more than any vegetables in Umbria; but if Nan mentioned the cypresses, or the pruning, or the stone urns which needed constant attention he would shrug – and swear, she thought – and stump away sullenly.

'Antonio is whistling,' she wrote to Graziella. Would the novelty of Perugia wipe out for ever the memories of the Villa Giulia, the cool spacious rooms, Maria's food, the roses, the meadow? Not the meadow, she thought, not the meadow.

'Antonio is whistling and I must go in to see about the breakfasts,' she wrote. She gathered up the discarded paper at her feet and rose and walked back to the house down the weedless path.

'In three days Lily arrives and perhaps we'll get back to normal,' were her first words to Aunt Dot who was already in the kitchen.

'Dr Fortuno's called. Molly Baghot's been taken ill.'

'Ill? Ill with what?'

'He didn't say. He wants you to go down.'

On the way to Signora Falcone's Nan posted the letter to Graziella. As soon as it fell out of sight she wished it back again, remembering its stilted phrases, its futile encouragements.

'Molly can't be ill now,' she said to Fortuno.

'I think it's appendicitis.'

Nan stared. 'But she's too old,' she cried.

'I'm afraid not. I'm waiting for a second opinion and then . . .' He led her upstairs. 'Hospital.'

'Can't you tell if it is or it isn't?'

'It isn't always easy. And she's a difficult patient. She's frightened at the thought of operations, hospitals . . . That's why I sent for you.'

Molly was in bed, grey and sweating. Signora Falcone stood by looking important, surrounded by bowls and water jugs and fiercely laundered flannels.

'It's been coming on for two days,' she wailed to Nan. 'Two. I said, "Signora, you look unwell. You should rest." But no. "It's indigestion," she says. "It will pass."'

'So it will,' said Molly in a cracked and furious voice from the bed. A fierce face poked between the starched sheets.

'We shall see,' said Fortuno, and put a hand over hers.

She was so tiny there seemed nothing of her beneath the bedclothes.

'We shall see, signora,' he repeated more softly.

'I won't go to hospital,' she cried.

'If you have to go, Signora Mortimer will be with you and you'll be quite safe.' He spoke in the gentle rhythmic tone he used with frightened children.

They heard the sudden drawing up of a car with relief. It was the second opinion.

'Not long now,' said Fortuno, still holding Molly's hands in his.

'Holy Mother, Perugia!' exclaimed Maria when Nan arrived back at the villa just after lunch.

'Couldn't Dr Fortuno operate in Cittavigile?' asked Aunt Dot.

'My sister,' said Pia, 'had her appendix taken out on the kitchen table.'

'It was felt best all round if she were taken to Perugia. She's old and frail.' Nan sat down wearily and took off her hat. Did she detect an atmosphere? 'They operated immediately. She looked like a doll on the trolley. I waited till Dr Fortuno came out and said everything had gone well and then came back here.'

Driving up the main road the Morris had jerked and spluttered – all-too-ominous signs of imminent expiry. Nan had willed the car along and willed herself back to the Villa Giulia. Why couldn't the appendix have waited until the end of the week, waited for England? she thought. Why should an aged appendix misbehave at all? She had intended to stop in Cittavigile to give Signora Falcone the news but the car was still misbehaving. She drove on.

At the villa Aunt Dot seemed firmly in charge. How could I ever have thought her incapable of managing Laburnum Lodge? Nan wondered. All the same, there was an atmosphere.

'The Greenways are leaving,' was Aunt Dot's first announcement.

'But they're booked in for another four days.'

'They're going on to Rome and then home. They seem disillusioned,' said Aunt Dot sadly. 'But a French couple rang to make a booking and I took it. Is that all right?'

'People coming, people going. So much laundry,' put in Pia.

'I've told them the laundry must go down to the village,' Aunt Dot said. 'Antonio can take it and bring it back when he goes to the convent.'

That accounts for the atmosphere then, Nan thought. However, there was also some dispute about peas.

'If there aren't enough we must buy some from Signor Umberti. He sells vegetables, doesn't he?' Aunt Dot had told them briskly.

'We've always done the sheets here,' Maria protested to Nan.

'Buy vegetables from Umberti!' cried Pia.

They waited. They expected her to save them from the shock of change.

'It all sounds very sensible,' said Nan.

'I want to get up,' said Molly fretfully.

'It's not allowed.'

'What would be the harm if I'm properly stitched up?'

Nan sat on the end of the bed. It was a room not unlike Graziella's at the convent: sparsely furnished, wholly functional. The foot of the iron cot dug into her back.

'You ought to rest.'

'Why? I feel fine.'

Molly's bright little eyes glared and glared. Every five minutes she would ring the handbell that was intended to bring a nurse at the run and now, because they were wise to her, she had to ring and ring before they answered. All she ever wanted was to get up.

She was not allowed proper food, the sheets were scratchy, the doctor was a fat man, falsely jolly, not her dear Dr Fortuno who was only allowed to pop his head round the door. She had a whole catalogue of complaints. How tiresome she is, thought Nan, and then felt instantly guilty, for she knew Molly could also be funny and charming and perfectly sensible.

'I've sent a telegram to Lily,' she informed her when she was allowed to speak.

'Damn Lily,' said Molly with feeling.

'She can't travel yet. Say . . . a week,' said Fortuno. He had found Nan hurrying away down the antiseptic corridors.

'We'll have to find room for her at the villa then.'

'Nan . . .'

The smell brought it all back. She felt suffocated with pain. Her face was white. She ignored his hand and kept walking, desperate to get into the hot raucous smelly street.

'Nan,' he said again, and there was enough urgency in that one syllable to make two nurses turn and stare, suppressing giggles, but Nan herself did not appear to be listening.

'I'll come again tomorrow,' was all she said, and plunged out of the doors without looking at him.

'I bullied and bullied and they let me get up,' said Molly on Monday evening. She was in a strange bed-wrapper, like stitched-together dishcloths, across the crumpled collar of which Nan could read: '*Ospedale di* . . .'

'You look fine.'

'I want to eat.'

'Perhaps they'll let you tomorrow.'

On the bedside locker was a vase of flowers. Nan, who had brought a bunch of Villa Giulia roses, looked at them curiously. They were shop flowers.

'They're from Graziella,' Molly said.

'Has she been in?'

'A boy brought them. A boy in a black leather jacket on a motorcycle, sister said. I was amazed. How does the poor girl know I'm here?'

'I wrote to her. Besides, Sister Angela has been praying for you and I expect she commanded Perugia and Rome and Naples and Reggio and all the other convents to pray too.'

'Praying for me,' mused Molly.

Who, Nan wondered, was the boy in black? And did the convent know about him?

'Mr Ruddock rang and said Lily would come at the weekend. You're to come home with me until you're fit enough to travel.'

'How lovely, dear. And where shall I go? I never got to Rome, did I? Rome would be lovely.'

Nan went to the door to find a nurse to deal with the roses. She had the dull feeling that foretells disaster. 'I think you'll have to miss Rome. You're probably going straight back to England with Lily.'

'Never!'

'Never?' asked Fortuno, stepping in. 'What is this "never"?'

'She's your sister,' said Nan. 'She wants to do what's best. She wants . . .' Something reminded her: Molly's own words. 'She only wants to make you happy.'

'Rubbish,' said Molly. 'She wants Edward's money.'

The nurses adored her but prayed daily for release from her constantly ringing bell. Once in exasperation they ignored it and came in later to find that she had fallen out of bed. After that, anxiety and guilt brought them at the gallop.

'How is she?' Fortuno would say.

'Much better,' they would reply firmly. Perhaps tomorrow he would relieve them of her.

'Sister Angela's prayers have been heard,' he said to Nan. 'She will be back to normal in no time.'

'I've had another telegram,' Nan said. My prayers are never answered, she might have added.

'Arrival delayed. L. Trewarden.' Fortuno turned the paper over as if, by some eccentricity of the Italian

166

postal service, there might be something more informative on the back. 'So what does it mean?'

'It means Lily isn't coming . . . yet.'

He put his lips together, considering. 'She is a most mysterious lady.'

'Perhaps, like poor Molly's son – or should that be, Molly's poor son? – she doesn't really exist.'

'But she must exist. This Ruddock says so.'

'I was only . . . Never mind. Why doesn't she come? Molly might have died.'

'What does Degnare say?'

'That when he rings the lines are very bad.'

'So they are.'

They were standing in the hospital corridor. Like twigs caught against the bank they stayed uneasily in the one place while life flowed on around them. In an English hospital, Nan thought, people would hurry less and there would be a notice saying 'Quiet Please'.

'So they are,' said Fortuno of the telephone lines, and Nan nodded in agreement, recalling a dozen ruined conversations, misheard dates, unnecessary confusions. 'Be careful,' and he put out a hand to save her from a trolley. 'Be careful,' and he guided her closer to the wall. Irrelevantly she thought: How lightly he spoke of the hill as an old execution ground. We inhabit different worlds.

'Nan?'

He's remembered not to call me Anna, she thought, and was a little disappointed because no one else, after all, had ever done so. She braced her back against the wall while another trolley passed and the old nausea suddenly overcame her. The smell of the hospital revived so many memories: the smell, the young nurses, the wheeled beds with their iron bars.

'Nan, you're trembling,' said Fortuno.

Aunt Dot asked Fortuno to stay to dinner after he had driven Nan home from Perugia.

'He must have a surgery.'

'He didn't say so, dear.'

'Why on earth do such a thing?' asked Nan.

'It's the least we can do after he brought you back.'

'There wasn't anything wrong with the Morris. It was only that I felt dizzy in the hospital.'

'Still,' and Aunt Dot looked her up and down as if she might divine the reason for the dizziness, 'that housekeeper of his is a dreadful cook.'

'Did Maria tell you that?'

'I suppose she must have.'

'She and the housekeeper once loved the same man.'

'And Maria married him?'

'Neither of them married him. He died. I forget how. It was all very dramatic. At least, it is when Maria tells it. But it's enough that the housekeeper once turned her eye on him. They haven't spoken except to insult each other for twenty years.'

'How interesting,' said Aunt Dot.

Maria, to show off both her abilities and her contempt for the housekeeper, prepared 'another meal fit for the Palazzo Andreone', said Nan. Or for Robin, she thought. Maria had always spoiled Robin, though he had never appreciated it. She had found the tall pale Englishman with his stick and his melancholy face a romantic figure. In the village she referred to him as '*Il professore*', for she had to give him a title and he was always reading, always, a pile of books by his chair, on the table, by the bed. If he wasn't walking on the hill with the signora he was on the terrace with his books, and in winter in the *salotto* with more books. '*Il professore* is better today,' Maria would say to the village, or: 'He's worse, he had a bad night.'

For his part Robin thanked her for small comforts: his coffee, a rug, an exceptional meal – and ignored her. The domestic staff were Nan's concern. Also he shrank from Maria always – so huge, so coarse, so raucous. She did not simply laugh, she shrieked with laughter. When she sang in the kitchen the house reverberated. When she dropped pans or when old Pia transgressed she swore 'like a Naples sailor', said Robin.

'When did you ever hear a Naples sailor?' asked Nan.

'Well, they're street words.' He was embarrassed.

'She comes from the streets.'

As Robin grew weaker so he grew more tolerant. Maria carried him his coffee every morning knowing it would not be touched, but he would smile and speak, asking her about the day, Antonio, Pia, the village. It was as if, for a while, her great energy revived his own. 'A dying man thinks of his mother,' Maria told Pia. There was nobody more motherly than Maria. Strange children would climb uninvited into her lap. Her harsh loud voice could drop to the sweetest tones in a cradle song, a nursery rhyme, a riddle. Now Robin said, 'Why isn't Maria singing?' or 'Maria's late with the coffee this morning.'

'What a splendid meal,' Aunt Dot congratulated Maria when it was over.

'It was nothing,' said Maria.

'But everything so perfect: the pasta, the fish, the vegetables . . . everything.'

'Anyone could do it,' said Maria.

On the terrace, in a corner away from her guests, Nan sat with Fortuno and waited for Aunt Dot to return.

Tonight Nan had tried hard with her appearance. I'll look my age, she had thought, studying herself in the glass. Instead she looked like a child trying to look grown-up. The pallor of the hospital which had so alarmed Fortuno was heightened by the blue shadows under her eyes. The coffee cup was not quite steady in her hand.

'I'll have to fetch the Morris,' she said.

'Only if you're well enough to drive.'

'Of course I'm well. It was just . . . Once, years ago . . .'

There was no need for her to go on. His quick mind had leapt at once, gathering what facts he knew to provide the answer he required. So *that* was what it was, he might have said.

'Was it so terrible?' he asked gently.

She thought of the long labour and the dead child, the callous nurse and the consultant who looked at his watch.

'Yes, terrible,' she said.

16

THE policeman said, 'We have let the man go,' and he shrugged to express the proper resignation to the disappointments of life.

'What man?' asked Nan. She had been on the front steps sweeping away the rose petals – Pia's job, but Pia's legs were worse than ever in spite of prayer, Antonio's lotion and unstinting sympathy all round.

'The man we were questioning about the young priest.'

'I didn't know you were questioning anyone.'

'His alibi was good. We let him go.'

'I see.'

We see shadowy reflections, distorted, incomplete, she thought, and behind each mirror is another and in each we glimpse a little of the truth but never all of it.

The policeman lingered on the bottom step as if he hoped to be asked in. But what for? she wondered.

'Was he from the village?' she asked at last.

'Not far away,' was the enigmatic reply.

'Was he in love with Graziella?'

'In love?'

'Then why did you question him?'

'He's the son of the man the priest's father betrayed.' He saw her frown. 'In the war,' he added and shrugged again.

'But he's had years to take revenge. Why now?'

'Perhaps now was the time,' said the policeman calmly. He picked one of the scarlet geraniums and stuck it whimsically in his buttonhole.

'Because he was jealous,' Nan persisted. 'Because of Graziella.'

'Because of . . .' and he patted the flower into place and prepared to take his leave. 'Who knows, signora?'

The photograph proved Aunt Dot had once been young and slender, had worn leg-o'-mutton sleeves and known a young man in a velvet smoking jacket.

'Johnnie something. Your mother was mad about him. He was more her age, younger than me.'

'Mother?' said Nan.

Alas, there had never been a photograph showing Evelyn with the innocent and expectant expression of seventeen. And one imagines tyrants to have been tyrants from the cradle. 'Mother?' cried Nan in astonishment and amusement and disbelief.

She thought of it again on the way to the village. Mother in love, she thought; but the idea was preposterous. She tried to imagine Evelyn under the cherry tree giving herself up to the dangerous kisses – only kisses in those days, surely – of Johnnie-in-the-smoking-jacket, but it was no use. There was never such a woman, she thought.

'And where is the lady from England? Signora

Baghot's sister,' asked Signora Falcone when Nan collected the last of Molly's belongings from the house opposite the bakery.

'She'll be arriving soon.'

'Soon!' and Signora Falcone shrugged, a shrug of supreme disbelief and indifference. 'Soon. Soon. Always soon.'

The light wind flattened Nan's dress against her bare legs. Crossing the square she struggled a little with the two cases. One was the Major's, full of his earthly requirements. She knew in her heart that Molly would hardly have cared if she had left it, if Signora Falcone had donated its contents to the missions, the orphanage, to the bric-à-brac stall on the market. As she put it down thankfully to open the car boot she thought: If Mother had died Father would have given all her things away at once; there would have been no trace left. She felt depressed, stowed the cases quickly, closed the boot on them with relief. Robin and I, she thought, hoping for some kind of consolation, Robin and I were happy . . .

After the baby she had folded in on herself. Everything reminded her, everything was pain. The days seemed unvarying except that they were punctuated by fewer of these debilitating moments – or sometimes more.

'You'll have to pull yourself together,' said Robin at last, running out of patience.

She had rejected him for months, fighting off his advances wildly as if he were a stranger, as if she feared him. He spoke to the doctor and the doctor explained to her that this sort of behaviour put marriages at risk.

'Because I can't sleep with him? I thought it was more than that,' she cried, 'marriage. I thought it was . . .'

The doctor recoiled. He did not let her finish. 'Severely depressed,' he told Robin. 'Give her a little more time.'

'Crises should unite, not divide,' she had told Aunt Dot, spent after one of the now-familiar seizures of weeping. 'He doesn't grieve for the baby. He doesn't think of her.'

'She was never real to him,' said Aunt Dot.

He felt her move in my womb, thought Nan. He saw me grow slow and careful, bending suddenly with a sigh when the child kicked. And yet it's true ... He didn't sweat and struggle for her life, nor did he see her dead, her perfect face, the tiny hands.

'But can't he understand how real she was to me?' she cried.

'We can have another child,' Robin said, and for his own sake and for hers he rushed her away to Italy and the green hill and the Villa Giulia 'and sun', said Aunt Dot, who believed implicitly in its healing powers.

'I'm afraid ...' said the English doctors.

'Never mind them. There'll be another baby,' Robin told her, but she was not ready for another even if it had been possible and by the time she was, Robin himself was ill and 'We must be careful,' he said, and his lovemaking had no trace of passion it it, only kindliness.

The sun beat on Nan's bare head. The inside of the Morris was too hot to bear. I'll have a drink, she thought, and turned towards the café, but there was Dr Fortuno by one of the tables talking to an old man. I must avoid him, she thought, though there was no reason why she must. Only he, like Molly, like Graziella, had been a disturbing influence this summer. I don't want to be disturbed, she said to herself. I want to live quietly. I want to live an ordinary quiet life.

What is an ordinary quiet life? she wondered. Like Aunt Dot's at Laburnum Lodge? But Aunt Dot was still visited by old friends from her days on the literary magazine, by poets and painters and people who sculpted 'the most tremendous things, twenty feet high' said Aunt Dot. She had encouraged the plumber to study philosophy, she had been so taken by his remarks on the geyser . . .

The hotel was a quiet life, Nan thought, before: before the Major died and Molly was set free like a genie from the bottle. People came and went, rarely any trouble, paying their bills and telling me how beautiful the house was, the views, Assisi, Perugia . . .

The car seemed exceptionally heavy and unwieldy today, like a tank, she thought grimly, fighting it through the narrow streets. All around there were cats and children, old women sitting in doorways, dirt, cleanliness, squalor, tidiness, windowboxes, washing, noise. Life, thought Nan. There's too much life. For a moment she felt overwhelmed. She remembered quiet summer days in Cambridge, the sound of water, of infrequent footsteps on gravel walks, of bicycle bells and ducks splashing under the willows.

Under the cypresses she stopped. I wish I smoked, she thought. She looked down at her hands, 'Not very well kept', she said aloud. Then, dramatically: 'My roots aren't in this soil,' she said, looking down the valley and across to the far hills. They've never been in any soil much, she thought with sudden insight. Cambridge, Kensington, Laburnum Lodge . . . There isn't anywhere, she thought. There isn't anywhere in particular. She was conscious of a pain, but where and of what kind she could not tell. It hurts, she might have said, like a child. But when she drove on and through the gates of the Villa Giulia the pain went.

This is as good a place as any to put down roots, she thought.

'You look as if you could do with a cup of tea,' said Aunt Dot when she stepped into the cool of the house, but it was not tea she brought, it was gin.

'Gin is your answer to everything,' said Nan, smiling.

'You look peaky.'

'That was Mother's word. She always tried to make me less peaky, to make me ... a swan,' said Nan, 'instead of the duckling I was.'

'Did Signora Falcone make a fuss?'

'Not much of one. She was glad to be paid, glad Molly isn't going back there.'

'I don't think Evelyn had much to worry about. You were just a late developer.'

'You keep changing the subject. And this is almost neat. I shall be rendered incapable,' and Nan glanced at the clock, 'at eleven in the morning.'

'I hope not. It was intended to fortify you. That fiery little nun is in the garden scorching about between the bushes. She wanted to talk to you, she said.'

'Sister Angela?'

'Such an unsuitable name. You'd think they'd be more careful since they name them when they're already grown up. It's not like babies when you don't know how they'll turn out.'

'I wish you'd told me before I drank the gin,' said Nan.

The garden was steeped in heat. The hedges were dusty and aromatic. On the stone seat the habited figure sat totally still, hands in her lap. When Nan drew near she saw that the nun's eyes were closed, and there were little blue veins criss-crossing the papery lids. A wisp of grey hair showed beneath the wimple that had become slightly disarranged during the long bicycle ride.

'Sister?' Nan hoped the fumes of gin would be dissipated before they reached the arched nostrils.

The eyes opened.

'What a beautiful garden,' said Sister Angela. 'If you close your eyes all you do is smell roses, roses . . .'

Afterwards they supported each other back to the villa like two old women. Like two infirm old women, Nan thought, which neither of us is. Sister Angela's arm was firmly linked in hers; her long skirts brushed Nan's bare legs.

'Nobody knows what to do for the best,' the nun had said. On the stone seat she had perched with a tremendous stiffness as if she had been brought up to sit straight. If nothing else the orphans had impeccable deportment. Had Sister Angela once been a convent orphan? Had she long ago been recruited by God from those ranks of pinafored girls hurrying to Mass across the square?

'She goes out whenever she can and meets all these . . . unsuitable people,' Sister Angela said.

Boys on motorbikes, thought Nan. 'I don't see how I can help.'

'She loves you. Perhaps she will talk to you.'

'I thought she'd enjoy Perugia so much once she'd settled, once . . .' But she seemed, from the worrying daily bulletins, to be enjoying it too much already.

'She looks on you as a sister, as a mother,' said Sister Angela. 'She would like to see you and . . . it might do some good.'

A sister and a mother, thought Nan. As she had schooled herself never to cry since those days when she had cried too much, her eyes grew hard and shining. She bent her head. I cried for Robin, she remembered, and thought of Dr Fortuno's wet shoulder, Maria's wet bosom, the wet pillows . . . Only that had seemed a small interlude in all these years of self-control. She blinked. Robin was right, she decided: I'm too sentimental, I'm too easily touched.

She had been touched in the hospital but then she had felt sick and faint.

'Nan,' said Sister Angela, and that was when she had stood up and taken Nan's arm and turned her towards the house. 'Dr Fortuno was right. You're not well. You've grown thin this last month and your eyes . . .' Sister Angela stared into her eyes. 'Yes, there are shadows. Aren't you sleeping? The doctor is anxious. He says you do too much, worry too much.'

'It's nothing. My legs feel a bit weak, that's all.'

It's the gin, Nan thought, horrified, and all the way back to the house she breathed religiously through her nose, in out, in out, while she leaned on Sister Angela and Sister Angela leaned on her.

'I don't know about nuns,' said Aunt Dot. She felt they represented the kind of sensationalism frowned on in her Low Church childhood. Her mother would have given them a frosty stare and hurried her children away as Evelyn had once hurried Nan past a rack of saucy postcards.

'She's completely at a loss,' Nan said. 'They're hinting in Perugia they would like her taken away.'

'After only a fortnight?'

'So much seems to have happened in that fortnight.'

'They should settle her with some nice family. Heavy discipline won't do any good at her age. The most they can do is find her a decent job and pray. They ought to be good at praying.'

'It seems to have worked for Molly.'

Long ago Aunt Dot had prayed for Nan but only in the unformulated way the non-religious use: let her be pretty, happy, clever; let her get away from Evelyn as soon as possible; let her meet people who bring some excitement into her life. Was I unheard because there was nobody to hear or because I didn't know whom to petition? she wondered later. She had never said 'Please God, let Nan be happy;' she had of necessity simply thrown the request haphazard into the ether. And Nan had remained plain, only moderately clever, nearly always vaguely unhappy, allowed 'suitable' friends under supervision. Even at nineteen, when she had developed – at last, it seemed to Aunt Dot – a rather surprisingly characterful face under that attractive hair, she had been reclusive. 'Ridiculously shy,' said Evelyn. She had not been shy at all. She had been quiet because Evelyn was assertive. She was not cowed, simply contained. 'It was that or spend all the time arguing,' she said, and by that time anyway she was handicapped: Evelyn was ill.

War came. 'I think it's better organized this time,' remarked Aunt Dot, queueing for rations; but like all passions it was disruptive. Nan announced that she had got a night job in a canteen and several times was caught in air raids, not returning till breakfast-time.

'I'm always alone and I can't manage,' Evelyn complained.

In Sussex Aunt Dot prayed for romantic solutions. London was full of men, young men in uniform, all sharing a little in the compelling aura of those daring death in a good cause. It was time Nan's emotions were tried by love, sex, separation. I suppose, in a way, I was answered, thought Aunt Dot unhappily. She had tried hard to approve of Robin and her failure left her at a loss. Now when Nan was apparently happy at last, how ironic that she must struggle against the instinct that said the marriage was a mistake. It was as if all her years as Nan's champion had been wasted: Nan had not wanted any of what she had hoped to give her.

It was in Italy the change had been wrought. 'Yes, wrought,' Nan might have said. 'Hammered, forged.' Strangely it had begun the day she had come to live here. 'How does one live in such a place?' she had asked, as if she saw possibilities that frightened and excited her. Robin's death had meant more blows, more knocks, more hammerings. 'Only the ordinary sort,' Nan would have said. 'Women lose husbands every day. And lovers. And children.' But the Nan who ran the hotel was not quite the same Nan who had run the house with only Robin and herself in it.

Major Baghot's death had been another blow. Why should that be? Nan wondered, when she had forgotten what he looked like – 'Well, he'd only stayed a night, or was it two?' – and even how they had arranged the funeral. This time, though, the blow cracked the shell. My shell, thought Nan. It had cracked a little when I lost the baby but I sealed up the crack quickly because of the pain. Now the crack was too big to do anything about. There was Graziella and Father Michele, Dr Fortuno, Aunt Dot, Sister Angela carrying me away to Perugia. A new Nan, she thought. 'The old one', said Aunt Dot when she thought about it. 'You were this Nan in the beginning before . . .' Before Evelyn's baleful influence, that first funeral, the unsentimental departure from the Cambridge house.

'My niece has gone to Perugia with Sister Angela,' Aunt Dot told Fortuno when he called at six. What a dear man really, she said inwardly and led him away to the terrace for gin and as much intimacy as he would allow her, which was considerable, for he spoke affectionately of his dead wife whose name, though she could not know it, had not been mentioned to anyone for years.

'What does Sister Angela hope for?' he asked at last, coming back to the subject they had started with and from which he had been led by the gin and Aunt Dot's flattering attention.

'Miracles, of course. She hopes Nan will turn Graziella back into a little girl.'

'Wants what?'

'Wants Graziella to be the innocent, obedient child she was.'

'That one was never an innocent child.'

'All right. Inexperienced child.'

'Perhaps she was never that either.'

The French couple who had replaced the Greenways were arguing loudly at the far end of the terrace. It was something to do with fish. Fortuno said slowly, 'It's impossible. She's a woman now. She may be pregnant.'

'Of course it's impossible. That's why I call it a miracle. But Sister Angela has to try. Her faith insists that miracles happen.'

'Ah well, they'll have a pleasant drive to Perugia. And the nuns there have a garden full of peach trees and apricots and figs. Unless . . . Nan never liked Sister Angela.'

'They seemed to be getting on very well in the garden,' remarked Aunt Dot.

★

Sister Angela had confined her veil with an elastic band. Nan realized how necessary this was when they turned on to the main road and the hot wind blew in through the open windows.

'I love speed,' said Sister Angela.

'The car's rather old,' and Nan watched the quivering speedometer needle for a moment. 'Everything will overtake us.'

Vegetable trucks overtook them, an oil tanker, two gesturing boys on a scooter, Sister Angela held down her scapular that threatened to fly up and smother her face. Because of the elastic band Nan could see more grey hair. She remembered seeing the novices with their overskirts tucked up, skipping in their petticoats. The orphans at the ends of the ropes had chanted in excited shrieks and sometimes great lengths of black-stockinged leg had been revealed as they deliberately turned quicker and quicker.

The sun was setting. Shall we eat at the convent in Perugia? she wondered. There was a dusty red glow everywhere, a warm blowy beauty.

'You must tell me the way,' she said as the city came in sight.

Go left, go right, round here, straight on . . . The small capable hands pointed and urged and explained as only Italian hands can. Left, right, the steering cruelly heavy, the gears stiff. Then there was a familiar-looking blank wall, 'another fortress' thought Nan, a door so small it could only have been meant as a deterrent.

'Here,' said Sister Angela. 'Stop here.'

They were admitted. The black veil, freed again, billowed a little in the warm breeze. They crossed a court, another. There were fruit trees on every wall. Inside there was a holy silence, spiced, as it should be, thought Nan, by the smell of good food and the pleasurable expectation of visiting sin. In a cool corridor a whole flock of nuns was congregated.

'They're going to chapel,' said Sister Angela. Nan was following a pace behind like a cup-bearer.

By the time they had drawn level with the chapel door, the singing had begun, piercingly sweet. How beautiful, thought Nan, and she must have hesitated, for she was plucked forward by Sister Angela's hand and found herself in some other passage, sweaty with life, noise, garlic, hot air. There were what looked like classrooms and what seemed a refectory with trestle tables and benches. The yelling of children was growing louder.

A figure was hurrying to meet them. She was tall, gaunt, harassed, and a small boy clung to her rosary.

'Sister Francesca, God be with you,' said Sister Angela formally. In Sister Francesca's hand was a white envelope. When she spoke she waved it gently, her voice low and somehow breathless and guarded, for the little boy was all ears, straining up to try to touch the mysterious letter.

Nan heard odd words here and there. Even now she had trouble with accents and Sister Francesca was from Calabria, 'where they hardly speak Italian' Pisan Father Pietro might have said. She heard 'This morning . . . Only this . . . Nobody . . . Authorities . . .'

'Nan?' Sister Angela turned to look into Nan's rapt face. Was she trying to hear the far-away singing in the chapel, so beautiful, so 'out of this world' as she told Aunt Dot when she tried to describe the visit, the building, the rows of nuns filing silently through chapel door. 'Nan, have you understood?'

'No,' said Nan. 'No, I haven't understood a thing.'

'Graziella has run away.'

'On the back of a motorbike,' Nan said afterwards to Aunt Dot.

To her surprise she found the envelope offered to her, courteously reversed by Sister Francesca so that she was able to read her own name perfectly clearly: Signora Mortimer, Villa Giulia, Cittavigile.

'Of course we haven't opened it,' said the nun.

When Nan made no move to take it she stepped forward, took Nan's hand and placed the envelope in it.

'It is yours, signora. Read it. It's from Graziella.'

17

GRAZIELLA began: 'Most kind Signora Mortimer.'
Could that be me? Nan wondered. She had never considered herself as particularly kind and she no longer
recognized Signora Mortimer, who seemed another
woman in some previous and almost forgotten existence.
The nuns had allowed her to sit in one of the empty
classrooms to read the letter but the door was ajar; she
was not alone. The soft footsteps passed up and down
and there were muffled voices and the click of rosary
beads. When she had finished reading, she felt compelled to go out and give them the news, 'except that
they already know it,' she said to herself.

'There's nothing to say where she's gone. It's just
goodbye,' she said. *Saluti affetuosi da Graziella.* 'One
day I will see you again,' she had written.

'The police may ask to see it, of course,' said Sister
Angela on their homeward journey.

'My letter? I suppose they might.'

In the darkness the nun was invisible. Occasionally a

white face between the bands of the wimple was illuminated by oncoming traffic. 'She'll come to a bad end,' she said sorrowfully.

'That's the sort of thing my grandmother used to say if she saw a girl wearing lipstick.'

'But this . . .' There were no words for Sister Angela's disappointment. 'I never thought . . . First a priest and then . . . then someone else so soon after.'

'I know. But there's nothing we can do. Even if you find her, what can you do?'

Though her heart ached she felt also something like relief. It's true, she thought: we can only pray. We can't arrange people's lives for them. Graziella has run away with the boy in the black jacket and that's that. And she remembered that the boy in the black jacket had carried a bunch of flowers to Molly Baghot.

'I expect it will be all right,' she said optimistically.

Sister Angela grunted and leaned forward to see if the next road sign indicated Cittavigile.

'Girls like that are always difficult,' she said.

Nan thought of Graziella in the kitchen at the Villa Giulia, lithe, alive, answering up pertly. 'Answering back', Maria would say. Had they been afraid of her ripeness? Or afraid for her, knowing the hazards ahead? 'Fourteen and already . . . that,' Maria had said when she had first come to work. 'That' encompassed everything: the small breasts, the slender thighs, the perfect face, the little white teeth that worried her bottom lip when she was puzzled, the modest expression that was belied by the searching, curious eyes. 'She looks at all the men,' Maria complained. 'Well, they look at her,' Nan had snapped. And then she remembered Father Michele calling Molly Baghot 'Signora Baggotta' and the way she had wondered how he spoke to Graziella, like a priest or like a man. The priest can't be separated from the man, she thought, and then: We go around with our eyes closed.

In the headlights she saw 'Cittavigile 2' and she thought she recognized a tin shack on the side of the road and the track to a farm.

'We are almost home,' said Sister Angela with relief.

The road twisted and turned. There were no lights. Even the village when they reached it seemed dark and sleeping. But that's ridiculous, thought Nan. The Morris nosed between the old battered walls. Then they were in the square and there were people everywhere, and noise and light. There were old men at the café, young men sitting under the trees, girls and older women walking arm in arm, children running in and out. The baker's three-legged dog and several cats fled in front of the car.

At the gate to the convent Nan waited politely while Sister Angela was admitted, then she turned the car and drove back up to the village, on and up again, past the sentinel cypresses, up, up to the villa. Her arms felt tired, her back ached. My head aches, she thought, surprised. She accelerated up the drive.

The house was all light. Even where the shutters were drawn upstairs light penetrated through cracks, between the boards. It looked welcoming and 'beautiful', said Nan, stopping and climbing out and almost falling into Aunt Dot's arms.

'How late you are,' scolded Aunt Dot. 'Poor Dr Fortuno went home hours ago. He told me all about himself. You know, he's a remarkable man.'

'I expect he is.'

'And how was Graziella?'

'Graziella has run away with the boy on the motorbike and the nuns are quite sure she'll end on the streets of Rome. I'm so tired. It was a dreadful journey back.'

Nan found herself in her own sitting-room with coffee at her elbow.

'Dr Fortuno was afraid of something like this.'

'You're right, he is remarkable. If he could have predicted this then he's very remarkable indeed,' Nan said. 'Did he stay to dinner *again*?'

'I could hardly send him away without asking.'

'He's neglecting his patients.'

'He came up after his surgery.'

'Why did he come?'

'To ask after you.'

He had come every day while Robin was ill until Nan could have screamed at him to go away. 'There's nothing you can do,' she wanted to yell. It would have been almost joy to yell and shout, to make 'an undisciplined noise' she said. But she said it to herself. In public she must behave properly. Fortuno came and went so regularly that he seemed to live in the house and she grew to hate him ... almost. Almost, she thought. He was always there, 'keeping up my spirits', said Nan, even when she would have liked, felt she desperately needed, to let them down.

What was worse was that he was everything Robin was not: emotional, provoking, tender, humorous, proud, touchy, short-tempered. He appeared always to know all about her, to be able to judge her moods, to choose the argument that would sustain her another day, another week. She had been astonished and then resentful. Robin had never known what moved her. How dare this strange man – for she thought of him as a strange man – have such powers?

'I wish he wouldn't,' she said to Aunt Dot. 'Ask after me. Make a fuss. What's the point?'

'Well . . .' said Aunt Dot, but there was nothing she could add that Nan would not find upsetting.

Nan shrank into her chair, easing off her shoes. Tomorrow there were more guests arriving, Maria to cajole, Pia to placate, Antonio to . . .

'I feel as if I've walked to Perugia and back,' she said. 'I wonder if I'm sickening for something. I seem to have a headache.'

'All those nuns, I expect,' remarked Aunt Dot consolingly.

Monsieur Armande had a small dog that barked incessantly and he gave Nan to understand that he did not care for Italian food. 'So I must get back before Maria has dismembered them both,' Nan told Molly, perching on the end of her bed and eating her grapes.

'People are so insensitive,' was Molly's comment. She pushed the bowl across the coverlet. 'Have them all, dear. The place is like a vineyard. That strange woman down the corridor gave me all hers before she went home.'

'You've been visiting, then.'

'Well, I shuffle about. The nurses all scold, of course. Dear Dr Fortuno made me promise to stay in bed and I do . . . do promise, I mean, but it's so boring: there's absolutely nothing to do, and all the staff are too busy to talk.'

The sun fell cruelly on the shrivelled animated face. We have to accept such ravages, Nan thought philosophically. Molly suddenly chirped, 'I've had a letter. Guess who sent it?'

'Most kind Signora Baggotta,' Nan read.

'Such a dear girl and so much in love.'

'Molly, you didn't . . . Did you . . .' Nan laid down the letter. 'You gave them your picnics,' she accused.

'Well, they were hungry,' Molly said, perplexed. 'Why ever shouldn't I?'

'And now she's run away with some boy she's only known ten days . . . She doesn't know what she's doing. But later . . .' Nan closed her eyes as if she might see the future, see beyond grief and guilt and the void of loss. 'I suppose she'll never go back to the convent,' she finished, opening her eyes on Molly's face against a background of hospital bed, eccentric electrical wiring and a holy picture. How could she go back? she thought, back to the knitted vests and the sensible shoes and the self-denial. They would give her baskets of mending to do, and cooking and cleaning and shepherding the little ones. They would find her a job with a good family but she would run off or return pregnant and defiant. The nuns would never know what to do with her. 'They're jealous,' Aunt Dot would declare with her deep distrust of nuns. 'They're afraid for her,' Nan might reply. They had always taught Graziella that if she held herself cheap so would the whole world.

'Oh,' gasped the little nurse who entered like a thunderclap, duster in hand. 'Oh signora! The grapes! Grapes everywhere. And they'll be here to inspect you in two minutes.'

Molly had found her teeth uncomfortable and was adjusting them. The nurse scooped at the loose grapes frantically.

'We've been celebrating my leaving,' Molly told her, having put her mouth in order.

'Leave? Not yet, signora,' and the nurse plunged under the bed, straightened, jerked the coverlet, smoothed out the creases where Nan had sat, tucked in a corner, dashed out.

'Sooner than she thinks,' announced Molly.

'Are you avoiding me?' asked Fortuno, joining Nan at the table.

'Of course not.'

'I hoped to see you in Perugia.'

Why? she wondered. 'Well, now you're seeing me in Cittavigile.' She tipped back her head and closed her eyes against the sun. She had chosen a table only half in shade. When it gets too hot, she had thought, I shall simply move round.

'They'll never find Graziella, you know.'

'No. I never thought they would.'

'I heard you had a letter.'

'So did Molly Baghot. I gave mine to the police.'

'They won't bother to look very hard. So many girls run away.'

'Don't boys?'

'A few. Perhaps not so often. How do they eat or get their clothes mended? At home everything's done for them.' He looked into her coffee cup, saw it was half full and raised his hand to call the waiter. Across the square the French couple from the Villa Giulia came in sight, arguing.

'Was she pregnant? Graziella. Was that why she went off with this boy?' Fortuno asked.

'I don't know.' There are so many things we don't know, she thought. 'I don't know if she was pregnant. She ran away . . . I think she felt she had to do something.' I started the hotel, she thought, Graziella ran away with a boy in a black jacket.

'*Cappucino, signore.*'

'*Grazie.*'

'*Prego.*'

The sound of strident French quarrelling, of footsteps on the cobbles, made a background to the nearer sounds of Fortuno stirring his coffee. Nan's eyes closed again. If I opened them and found myself back in Sussex would I mind? she wondered. She strained after memories: the bitter smell of cut privet, the drum of rain on the conservatory roof, the ting of a bus bell. Instead she saw Evelyn's face on the raised pillow, the sudden surprised look the moment before she died, and she heard the nurse's firm no-nonsense voice saying, 'How I prefer no pain at the end, just a nice fading away,' as if someone else might prefer agony and convulsions for choice.

'Nan, are you awake?' Fortuno touched her arm.

'How can you bear to work in hospitals?' she asked, and then: 'I'm sorry. That was a silly thing to say. I ought to get back. There are more people arriving for dinner and there's Molly's room to prepare. Are you sure she's all right? She looks so thin.'

'She won't eat the food they give her.'

Nan sighed. She felt burdened by other people's struggles like a mother whose grown-up children have suddenly returned, demanding and unreasonable. She said: 'I wish . . .'

'What do you wish?' He leaned forward. Was he genuinely interested, then?

'I wish Lily were here already. I wish Graziella . . .' But after all it seemed childish to hope that the boy on the motorbike was much different from most boys at that swaggering age. 'Oh, I don't know. If wishes were horses beggars would ride.'

Fortuno smiled, uncertain. 'Beggars?'

'Communication is such a problem, isn't it?' said Nan.

'They're all aromatic,' said Aunt Dot, surprised. She had walked down the garden to see why Maria was so long talking to Antonio and had brushed in and out of all the little bushes, distracted by the perfume of roses, some plants that looked like lilies, the velvet shade under the trees. 'Aromatic,' she said again, holding crushed leaves under Maria's nose.

'But of course.' Maria stared. Was it conceivable that any woman with a garden of her own did not recognize myrtle?

Today Aunt Dot was wearing a dress with spots the size of pennies and a hat like a Chinese coolie. 'Is this the latest fashion?' Evelyn had always asked scornfully on seeing her. 'It's mine,' Dot would retort. 'Don't grow like your Aunt Dorothy, for God's sake,' Evelyn had commanded Nan. 'Gin and cigars, married men . . .'

'Aunt Dot is fun,' Nan told her schoolfriends. 'She always does exactly as she likes. She runs a magazine.'

For nearly thirty years she had edited a highly regarded literary 'rag', as she called it. 'Oh, I know my readers,' said Aunt Dot and kept it going by force of personality, by force. 'I got on by doing, not thinking,' she told Nan. Had she stopped to think she might have thought of the bank account, the restless printers, the typists who 'really couldn't manage another month, Miss Procter, on such wages'. So she did not think, she did, and the girls stayed and the presses rolled off the precious pages. When she gave up they all said, 'Nobody could follow Dot,' and nobody did. The magazine wrote a flattering article about her – 'obituary', said Aunt Dot – faltered and closed.

At Laburnum Lodge she only enhanced her reputation for action. Within a fortnight the house was re-arranged and a tenant was in. 'The gutters need doing,' she wrote to Nan, though what needed doing to gutters was more than Nan knew or cared in those days. When Evelyn died she brought a spray of chrysanthemums from the garden to lay on the coffin, though to the best of Nan's knowledge the garden at Laburnum Lodge was an oblong of tired grass, an old apple tree and a thicket of laurel and privet.

Maria was talking about myrtle. She sounded as if she was saying a recipe out loud. Her voice rose and fell as if she was mentally reading line after line: and then add so and so and stir, and then put it to boil for two minutes, and then ... Or was it simply the natural cadences of Italian?

'*Scusi*,' said Aunt Dot, bewildered.

Usually they communicated so well, but today Maria was cross. When she was cross she refused to speak English. It had something to do with Antonio. Perhaps he had failed to produce the right vegetable at the right moment. Great cooks are temperamental, Aunt Dot reminded herself. I was only temperamental over Nan.

'I don't want her mixing with your literary crowd,' Evelyn had said. 'Heaven knows what they all do.'

'They rub along as best they can like most people. But Nan's seventeen, Evie. It's time she grew up a little.'

'She's still a child, an innocent child.'

'And by God, you're going to see she stays one.'

'She's been nicely brought up. I don't want her suddenly mixing with your raffish crowd.'

'Raffish,' repeated Dot. 'What a delightful old word. Is that what they are? Dear Evie, if she comes to stay with me she'll meet all sorts and it'll do her the power of good.'

'So I didn't stay with you,' said Nan later, still feeling the shadow of that old disappointment.

'Evelyn couldn't risk it.'

'But they were only writers, artists . . .' began Nan. Some, she knew, had been famous. 'They weren't wild animals.'

'Some were my good friends. But Evie always disapproved of my friends.'

'She disapproved of mine,' Nan said.

The blanket of Evelyn's disapproval had smothered her life and she had just struggled free when . . . 'Robin came along with cotton wool and packed her up again,' said Aunt Dot to Ivy.

Maria said irritably, 'What was it you wanted, signora?'

'Oh nothing. Just interfering. At my age what else is there for me to do?'

It was a relief to turn in at the gate. Then Nan saw Antonio picking the dead heads from the geraniums in the stone urns.

'Everybody's out,' he told her, rubbing the side of his nose the way he did when caught out in something she was not supposed to know about. 'Everybody.'

'But it's the middle of the afternoon. And why are you doing . . . this?'

'I was on my way for a sleep but I saw the petals,' and he showed her a handful of crumpled brown. 'And you were out. Everybody was out.'

'Out where?'

'Maria has gone to the village to see her cousin with the new baby. Pia has gone to Umberti's for more oil –

always more oil, so much oil. The old Signora Dorotea has gone for a walk with Giuseppina to the holy well.'

'A walk?'

'The English do not mind the heat,' he said, and dropped the dead petals into the bucket on his arm.

Nan thought: I've never had the house to myself. She ran up the steps like a girl, throwing her hat on the table by the telephone, flying upstairs, down, into the *salotto*. She dropped her linen jacket on a chair, kicked off her shoes, took glass and *acqua minerale* from the kitchen and carried it to the terrace. Tomorrow there might be Lily and Molly Baghot and the police about Graziella and Fortuno feeling pulses and Aunt Dot trying out school French on the unreceptive Monsieur Armande, but now, now this minute ... She leaned back, the glass cold and wet with condensation in her hand, her feet up on the low wall. The sun fell through the vine leaves and warmed her upturned face. Now I'm alone, she thought.

'It isn't a good time to call,' said Father Emilio humbly. He had surprised her looking beautiful and felt at a loss for words.

'No, it isn't,' she agreed.

'I've had a letter from Graziella.'

Nan's eyes opened but she did not look at him. She only moved her head to sip the water in her glass. She did not remove her bare feet from the top of the wall.

'She sent me money, signora, to put flowers on Don Michele's grave.'

Nan felt her throat constrict. She looked at the tiny bubbles in her glass. 'I hope you will. Put the flowers there, I mean.'

'Do you think I'd refuse?'

'You might think it unsuitable.'

He came closer, drew up a chair. She heard his skirts sigh as he sat and the creak of the old wicker. A faint smell of incense came to her and tomatoes and cigarettes.

'Your opinion of me is very low.'

'I think it is.'

He was silent. He looked up the gravel path and saw that it had been weeded, the hedges cut. The stone seat was just visible in its encircling bower of roses, a seat for lovers, 'though lovers never sit on it', Nan could have told him.

'No woman has ever loved me,' he confessed abruptly. 'No one will put flowers on my grave.'

'You aren't supposed to mind that. You're supposed to concentrate on heavenly rewards, not earthly ones.'

'You sound angry. Sometimes it is hard to concentrate exclusively on heaven.'

She opened her eyes again and turned her head to look at him. Then she smiled and the smile was wide and friendly and delightful and made her more beautiful, he thought, than he had ever expected. But she said, 'Surely you don't expect me to feel sorry for you?'

'I expect nothing. Only that you think of me a little more kindly.'

'Does my opinion matter?'

He smoothed the black skirts over his knees as if preparing himself to rise to a challenge.

'I've missed our wine-tasting,' he said.

18

'WHY is Lily coming?' demanded Molly. 'Lily's never wanted to come to Italy.'

This morning she was querulous, suddenly grown old. It was as if she could resist no longer: the confinement, the food, the lack of interest. 'She's not really herself,' the sister warned Nan. 'All I can get out of her is that she had a bad dream.'

Whatever the dream had been, Molly was reduced and feeble. Perhaps it had been of Lily, bullish and bullying. Since Nan had crossed the threshold she had talked of nothing else.

'Lily would never come to Italy.'

'She's coming to fetch you, to see you safely home.'

Molly's fingers plucked and plucked at the covers. Her face creased with vague alarm. 'Home?'

'Calne,' said Nan. 'You have to go and live in Calne.'

'But I have a son, you know. If you write to him I'm sure he'll come at once. *He* wouldn't take me to Calne. He'd take me to Rome.'

'I expect he would,' said Nan. She added quickly, 'Everything's ready for you at the villa. I've put you both in the big twin at the front. You can see the drive and all the cypresses.'

'How sweet of you,' said Molly without interest.

Besides the dream she had been troubled in the night by cramp in both her legs. To cure it she had walked along quiet corridors, passed through forbidden doors and come to rest in some far wing where an outraged sister had seized her like a housebreaker. She had been escorted back and lectured for some time. 'I didn't understand a word,' she told Nan. She could not, though, have misunderstood the meaning. 'But never mind, Dr Fortuno said he'd call today.'

'He calls nearly every day.'

'Does he? Time makes no sense in this place.'

'He's very busy. There's measles in the village.'

'I talk to him about you.'

'You shouldn't do that.'

'But he likes it,' said Molly.

'*Poverina*,' said Maria. 'How terrible to be old.'

'I sometimes think . . .' But Nan felt she ought not to say: I sometimes think Molly does it for effect, when she's bored, when no one's taking notice of her, when anyone mentions Lily.

'Good days, bad days,' and Maria tipped a heap of parsley on to the table. 'The brain dies little by little.'

'I sent another telegram,' said Nan.

'Telegrams! They fly here, then they fly there. How many times do we get ready for this Lily? Four, five, twenty? I tell you, signora, this Lily will not come.'

Which might be as well, Nan thought, unable to imagine these two old ladies living any kind of congenial life together. She took up a knife and began to chop the parsley and soon the pungent smell had driven out the thought of Molly and her sister, of Monsieur Armande's little dog that had stolen the rolls from the breakfast tables, of Graziella stepping out of the small door in the wall and on to the back of a motorbike.

'Signora?' Maria thought she was dreaming. The knife had fallen still. 'Look, you must chop it fine. Like this. This.' She gave a swift brutish demonstration. Nan nodded. 'Like this?'

Maria grinned approval. 'Quicker. Quicker, signora.'

Maria thought her new mistress grave and timid, like a child only newly conscious of the conventions of adult life.

Pia said, 'She doesn't know anything.'

'She can learn,' said Maria.

When she gave orders they could hear the pleading note in Nan's voice. She seemed tentative, a little mystified. Maria said, 'She's foreign. To her it's all new and strange.'

'Perhaps they will have children,' said Antonio. 'Children make women brave.'

'Perhaps,' Maria replied and shooed him from the kitchen. In those days she was brusque with him and never encouraged him to linger. She thought him uncouth. He could be neither cajoled nor driven. 'He is a peasant,' she said with contempt to old Pia. Then she began to appreciate that his artistry in growing vegetables was akin to hers in cooking them. When Robin fell ill she softened even more, passing on the latest news when he came up to the house each morning. 'He's better,' she would say. 'He ate something for breakfast.' Sometimes: 'He has a fever. The signora sat up all night.' Antonio made few comments but he drank it all in; she could see him slowly coming to conclusions. He liked Robin, who knew nothing about gardens and could only praise and admire. Besides, he was too old to keep changing masters. As time went on and early optimism was dulled he took to saying, 'Well, whatever God wills,' every time he came in or went out.

He exasperated Maria but in a necessary alliance to tempt Robin's fading appetite they drew together. She commiserated with his lack of wife and children, spoke respectfully of his war wound and, more practically, dug out his splinters; he was sorry for her widowhood, the death of her daughter in childbirth, the sons emigrated to America. She made him cough syrup for the winter; he reciprocated with a secret recipe for 'bad legs'. Old Pia had 'bad legs'. 'What is a poor old woman to do?' Pia was always complaining. 'My legs have never been good. Never.' Maria said to Antonio, 'If her legs get worse she'll do even less work and then what?' so he arrived next day with the bottle, the fabled cure.

Nan found them bent together over Pia's blotchy ankles.

'If there's anything wrong,' she said, shocked into the sternness she never usually managed, 'we must fetch Dr Fortuno. He's only upstairs.'

'Doctors cost money,' Pia said sulkily. She grabbed away the bottle defensively.

'But I'll pay,' said Nan.

'There's nothing wrong,' protested Antonio rather belatedly. He looked guilty as if caught in the act of murder. He suspected that a sharp medical eye might dismiss or covet his remedy, one or the other. Either would be calamity.

But Nan was aroused. For the first time they saw the

woman beneath the quiet dutiful wife, the hesitant mistress. The woman was strong and determined.

'There's trouble coming,' said Antonio.

Nan fetched Fortuno to the kitchen. Pia was still sitting on the chair, looking scared. Fortuno put his bag on the table and she looked at it in horror. But he knew what to say. 'You always seem to know what to say,' Nan said to him afterwards. He sighed over Pia's legs and shook his head. 'So bad. And like this all your life?' and then congratulated Antonio as he sniffed at the bottle: 'Your mother's recipe? Good. It must do wonders.' Then he caressed Maria's arm, turning her away, dropping his voice: 'You know, you must humour the mistress. She sits up all night, she barely eats, she tries to be strong. Don't give her these things to worry about.'

'There,' he said to Nan outside. 'I've pacified the outraged servants. Why don't you stay out of the kitchen? It only causes upsets.'

'You're laughing at me.'

'Of course. Couldn't you see you startled them almost to death?'

'You did nothing. What was in the bottle?'

'I said what they wanted to hear.'

'That was cowardly.'

'Or sensible.'

'But what was in the bottle?'

'Holy water, herbs. Who can say? Nothing harmful.'

'But if Pia's legs . . .'

'If her legs were perfect what would she have to grumble about?'

After that every morning Nan would ask Pia, 'How are the legs?' and Pia would reply, '*Bene, grazie, signora*,' and would report to the kitchen: 'She's so tired, so tired, but she asked after my legs. She's a kind woman after all, the signora.' And Nan thought: I've learnt my lesson. Strangely, instead of making her more deferential than before, it had made her bolder. She did not stop going into the kitchen but when she did she showed more interest. Only with Antonio did she continue to fail until the episode of the basket of vegetables. 'I learnt that lesson too,' she told herself.

'Are you looking after her?' asked Father Emilio. 'You must get her to eat.' He made it sound like a holy command.

'We do our best,' said Maria.

In adversity the household united. Young Father Michele brought flowers from the village on market days and Maria arranged them tenderly. 'He is a good boy,' she said dotingly to Nan. 'The signora thanks you,' she always said formally to Father Michele. A priest must be pure and yet know everything about the world, she thought. Her own sons at twelve had known more than this innocent. She saw him look at Graziella: shy adoration. 'God save us,' prayed Maria.

'Do you think the signora prays?' he asked.

'She prays every hour,' retorted Maria. 'She prays that the signore will live.'

'God knows what is best for us all,' said Father Michele cryptically. It was what Father Emilio was always telling him. He dared to say it to Nan, though her white face frightened him a little; he felt the inadequacy of mere words. In the silence he thought he heard a voice say, 'Are you sure He knows?' but Signora Mortimer had not spoken – she only stood and looked at him with such sad eyes in her pale, pale face.

Nan talked to Robin, read to him, watched him sleep. 'There is no God,' she felt like saying to Father Emilio and Father Michele. Once, tried by a stormy interview with Fortuno, she had referred to the priests as 'black crows'. She regretted it at once. 'They're kind to come every day,' she said to Maria; one or the other every day. Other people came but Robin was too ill to see them. Sometimes there were gifts. The convent sent peach preserve, Guiseppina and Graziella, who was just fourteen. 'It would help us,' Sister Angela said, 'and it would help you, signora.'

The day Robin died it was Signor Arletti who carried the news to the village because it was paper day at the Villa Giulia and Maria had told him at the kitchen door. He went straight back down the hill. 'The Englishman died this morning,' he announced. 'Don Emilio was with him.'

'And how is the young signora?'

'She is distraught.'

She was distraught for a moment, her face in Fortuno's shoulder, but after that . . . 'It isn't natural,' said Maria. Then came the brief breakdown. '*That* is natural,' said Maria. But in so short a time the villa became a hotel. 'Guests!' trumpeted Maria, fiery with anxiety. Old Pia retired because her legs could not stand the pace. In her place Graziella and Giuseppina giggled and whispered and skimped and charmed. I don't think I can manage, thought Nan again and again, but she managed. 'I muddled through,' she told Aunt Dot much much later. I muddled through with my eyes closed, she thought, until the Major died. Then what happened? I grew more muddled . . . but alive?

And: 'She has no idea,' Maria told Pia, 'even how to chop parsley. A simple thing like that!' but it was not real scorn, it was affection.

'She always remembers to ask about my legs,' said Pia.

*

It was a very small photograph in a folding silver frame. The woman was tall and slender and the two girls had been arranged at her feet with hats and sunshades. The younger was blurred and a little faded; only her determined jaw made any impression. The other was looking sideways at the camera and it seemed as if she might, secretly, be laughing.

'It was so long ago,' said Molly. 'We posed for hours. Mother said Lily was pulling faces.'

'Was she?'

'Oh yes. She wanted to go in and have tea.'

'Messing about only prolonged the agony then,' said Nan unsympathetically.

'Lily always liked to be the centre of attention.'

Molly put away the photograph. She was wearing that same hospital dressing-gown – where was her own? – that looked as if it had been sewn by convicts. Her hair was untidy. 'I don't know how you've put up with me,' she said, bowing her head. She was the picture of helpless frailty.

'I'll be glad when you're back at the villa,' said Nan.

'Will you, dear?'

Nan looked about helplessly. 'So many flowers,' she said. Every receptacle the hospital had been able to muster from two floors was full of blooms. It was as if every bouquet delivered in the past twenty-four hours had been diverted to Molly's room. Like a funeral, thought Nan suddenly – but there were chocolates too, and mysterious objects in hastily torn wrappings.

'Has everyone given you a present?'

'They're all so glad to be rid of me.' Molly's eyes sparkled with the old mischief. Nobody had lectured her today. They had all kissed her withered cheeks – even the fat hearty doctor she disliked – and had told her quite convincingly that they would miss her. Even patients from the wards – 'Where she should never have been in the first place,' said the sister severely – came in with offerings or sent them by some shy young nurse.

Nan thought of the photograph, of Lily's determined young jaw. She thought of the cruel but sensible fetters of the Major's will. She thought of Calne in the rain, wet dogs, cigars, old enmities. Oh Molly, she cried silently. As with Graziella she felt powerless. It was the absolute powerlessness of motherhood. One could not guarantee good behaviour, common sense, an easy passage, happiness; one could only love and worry, left out, left behind. She felt suddenly breathless with forebodings.

'I'll see you early tomorrow,' she told Molly. 'Did I bring all the right things?'

'Everything. Lovely.'

'It won't be long.' The words meant nothing; they were just noises. Nan's throat ached.

Molly had come to the door and there Nan had seen that the dressing-gown was really a child's and even on Molly was too short so that fragile and mottled bare legs showed between the hem and the absurd fluffy mules. Nan stooped, smelled old-fashioned rouge, had the sensation of kissing a dead leaf, felt brittle little bones clutching her hand.

'Goodbye, dear. Do be careful in that dreadful old car.'

On the way out the sister said cheerfully, 'She's a marvellous old thing really. She'll be like a little girl tomorrow, Signora Mortimer. She can't wait to go home.'

Nan nodded, not pausing, hurrying down the corridors to the sunlight, the fresh air. Driving back to

Cittavigile she tipped the rear-view mirror and saw how red her eyes were, how tight and shiny and ugly her face was where she continually wiped away the tears.

But why am I crying? she wondered.

The stone seat was romantic but uncomfortable for longer than a brisk exchange of kisses. Nan could feel the chill of it as she sat watching the night fall.

'Go away,' Aunt Dot had said. 'Go and have some time to yourself.' She had thrust a glass of wine between Nan's fingers and propelled her down the terrace steps.

Out here the domestic sounds of the house faded away. Tomorrow Lily would arrive in a taxi and Dr Fortuno would bring Molly back from the hospital in Perugia . . . But that was tomorrow, thought Nan.

'Good evening,' said Fortuno, coming from the meadow.

Because she was still thinking of Molly she said at once, 'Do you ever quarrel with your sister?' because she knew he had one, an elegant woman married to a judge.

'All the time.' He came to sit beside her.

'Were you skulking in the meadow?' she demanded.

He did not understand 'skulking'. 'What an ugly word,' he said. 'I was smoking, thinking.' He would have liked to tell her that Claire had written again. 'Again,' he wanted to say. 'You were right after all.' After all he had only wounded where he had hoped to give pleasure. And for a little while, he knew, letters would follow each other like the cries of the drowning, growing fainter, hope and strength fading together.

'I made that girl unhappy,' he confessed.

'Yes,' said Nan.

'How strange, when it was you I wanted to make unhappy.'

Nan was looking at the house, black against the deepening sky, yellow light in all the downstairs windows.

'I don't understand.'

She was not trying to understand. She felt immensely weary. The nagging fears for Molly, Graziella, even Aunt Dot, had used up all her energy. The wine too slipped down, anaesthetizing thought.

'I hoped you might be jealous,' Fortuno was saying.

'Might be what?'

He stirred impatiently, only half amused. 'You're not listening.'

'I'm sorry.' She stretched her eyes, shook her head. She couldn't remember what he had just said.

'Anna?' He had forgotten to call her Nan, or he did not want to. 'Anna, what are you thinking about?'

'An English garden.'

'Very beautiful?'

'Quite ordinary.' She could remember the rather unsuccessful rose beds, the listing croquet hoops. She could remember her father, leaning on his mallet, saying, 'I wish . . .' and breaking off, laughing at himself. He wished I could always be safe and happy, thought Nan.

'You're homesick for England,' Fortuno hazarded.

'My home is here.'

He took her hand, uncurled the defensive fingers and bent to kiss the palm. The gesture was as eloquent as it was astonishing. Nan felt herself grow hot.

'Anna, I love you,' he said and sounded as if he too was surprised.

He says these things to any woman fool enough to listen, thought Nan, but if her other hand had not held the wine glass she might have touched his dark head.

There was the crackle of footsteps between the myrtles.

'I've brought the bottle,' announced Aunt Dot. 'Darling, I can't see a thing. Where are you?'

'Oh dear, did I interrupt anything?'
  'I'm not sure.'
  'His goodnight was very brusque.'
  'He's brooding over Claire Prescott.'
  'And what are you brooding over?'
  'Everything,' said Nan.

19

Nan and Aunt Dot sat on the stone seat. All around them were rose buds.

'So many,' exclaimed Aunt Dot. 'It flowers and flowers.'

The morning coolness soothed them; there was the muted clucking of the hens behind the wall and the thin notes of little birds in the trees. Even Maria was not yet up; the kitchen was clean and empty, breakfast trays on the sideboard.

'I wondered what you were doing,' said Nan. 'I looked out of the window and saw you and thought you might be ill.'

'If I were ill,' asked Aunt Dot reasonably, 'would I walk in the garden?'

'I don't know.'

'This has been a lovely holiday, Nan dear, but . . .'

'But?'

'I must go home.'

'You could stay. We could sell the Lodge.'

'Sell the Lodge? Is that what you really want?'

'I thought it might be what you wanted. I wondered if you wanted to give up, give up the house, give up tenants, give up . . . the struggle with the geyser.'

'Not yet, dear,' said Aunt Dot.

The first notes of song wafted from the kitchen court-yard. 'That sounds promising,' remarked Aunt Dot happily. 'I would have gone home last week, you know, but I did so want to meet Lily.'

'So do we all,' said Nan.

Before Fortuno called to take her to Perugia to fetch Molly, Nan thought she would unpack Molly's case. Giuseppina should have done it but Giuseppina was missing Graziella and was sulky, 'and when she's sulky she's slow,' Nan said to Maria.

All Molly's dresses were grey or beige; all her shoes were suitable for long days on grouse moors. Signora Falcone had not taken much care and at the bottom was a tumble of underwear and stockings. Nan whisked out and put away automatically, her mind on other things. She emptied the case, stooped for a last time to put a handkerchief sachet in the chest of drawers, and something small and hard fell out with a little rattle and rolled away.

She knew what it was before she picked it up. How did I know? she wondered. It was a small brown glass bottle and the words on the label, though scribbled, were words she recognized. Dr Fortuno had spoken them, and the Perugia pathologist, and the Commendatore of police.

But these were lost in Florence, thought Nan, turning the Major's heart pills over in her hand.

★

Though the morning was still young the heat was intense. There was a fragrance of dry fields and vine leaves and petrol.

Fortuno said, 'They wouldn't have kept him alive.'

'But he should have taken them.'

'Anna, pills couldn't have saved him.'

'She hid them and pretended they were lost.'

'You don't know that.'

'Maria said at the time . . .' But what exactly had Maria said at the time? 'It was all that walking, walking. She tired him out . . .'

'You know how she is.' Fortuno's gesture was eloquent. 'Perhaps they *were* lost. Perhaps she forgot them. Perhaps, perhaps . . . Who knows?'

'She said it was a happy release.' Nan was haunted now: stray words, phrases, fragments of conversations came back to her.

'Anna.' He tried again. He even lifted his hand from the wheel briefly to touch her own clenched tightly on her knee. 'Anna, she didn't murder him.'

'I suppose not,' and she looked out, seeing nothing, or rather seeing only the body so decently composed under the bedclothes, Fortuno drawing up the sheet. At last, in a flat voice, 'What shall I do with the pills?' she asked.

'Give them to me. I'll dispose of them at the hospital. But I'll tell the Commendatore. Otherwise . . .' and he overtook a lorry, accelerating ostentatiously. 'I don't want to be accused of tampering with evidence.'

'But you said there hadn't been a crime,' said Nan.

The natural human response to a situation out of control is to retreat. Nan and Fortuno retreated only as far as the Sister's office in which, they had been assured, was a telephone they were welcome to use.

'I'm not happy about this,' Fortuno remarked over his shoulder to any interested onlooker, and since panic had set in half an hour ago, blame apportioned and refuted with vigour, voices raised, the nurses defiant or cowed by turn, even the cleaners involved, it was pouring oil on fire.

'You shouldn't have said that,' Nan remonstrated. 'It isn't really anybody's fault.'

'Nobody's fault that a sick old lady calmly walks out from hospital into a strange city without anyone asking where she's going?'

'But she isn't ill,' protested Nan. 'And she had a right to go, didn't she?'

Molly's departure had not incensed Fortuno so much as the unconcern of those who had watched her go. She had dressed, had packed up her night things, her toothbrush, the presents, the boxes of chocolates, had kissed goodbye all those she met in the corridor, and had simply wandered away to the main entrance encumbered by luggage and flowers.

'She has no money,' remarked Fortuno furiously. He was furious because he was undecided as to whether this was a good thing or a bad.

'She might have a little,' said Nan, remembering the notes she herself had pressed on Molly at Signora Falcone's, and the more recent loan 'so I can give something to the nurses, dear'.

'How much?'

'I don't know.'

Fortuno was dialling the Commendatore. 'How much, Anna? Can you guess?'

She shook her head. She had sat down on a hard chair and was leaning forward, her face in her hands. She might have been fainting or weeping but past experience cautioned him. He put out a hand and touched her shoulder.

'You're laughing,' he accused.

The laughter rose and engulfed her. She could no longer keep it decently hidden. She rocked forwards like a child, her coppery hair swinging against her cheeks, tears squeezed from her eyes. He could not help grinning. Then the phone buzzed in his ear. A voice put questions, staccato, peremptory.

'Anna, for God's sake. How much?'

She rubbed her knuckles in her eyes. She had not laughed like this for years. All morning she had felt somehow strapped in by disappointment, shrunken, anxious. She had thought she could not bear to think of Molly actively hastening the Major's death. Surely Molly could not do such a thing?

'Enough . . .' she began. The laughter was reaction and release. It began again, more feebly, and hurt her chest. 'Enough for a ticket to Rome, I expect,' she told Fortuno. 'She wanted to go to Rome.'

They came out into the hot streets and went to the centre of the town, to a café.

'She planned this,' said Nan. She had no strength left and felt remarkably peaceful.

'When I think . . .'

'Don't think. Perhaps they'll never find her.'

'Of course they'll find her.' His face was still dark.

Nan leaned back. The air was warm, eddying in mysterious currents in the angles of the old buildings. There was such noise, footsteps, shrill voices, argument, hooting. The cups clinked down on the metal table, Fortuno's voice seemed muted and indistinct and there was a sudden rattle of coins on a tray.

'Did you say you loved me?' Nan asked.

'What? This is hardly the place . . .' Fortuno's hands, poised above his cup unwrapping a lump of sugar, were apparently arrested in mid-air, paralysed.

'Why isn't it? Can you only say such things on the stone seat or under the cherry tree?'

'Anna . . .'

There were old men at the next table whose conversation, like Fortuno's hands, was suspended. They stared openly at Nan, entranced, willing her to continue.

'But it's either true or it isn't. Or is it only true in the dark, at one particular moment?'

'Don't be absurd.'

Over his shoulder, beyond the old men, beyond the young girls going by in pairs with ice creams, the children calling for their photographs to be taken, the old women, Nan saw a boy in a black jacket astride a casually leaning motorbike, a girl in slacks on the pillion, her arm laid lightly over his shoulder.

'It isn't her,' she said aloud.

'What isn't?' Fortuno followed her gaze but saw nothing.

'She'll write to me,' Nan stated with a certainty she no longer felt about anything.

'Molly?'

'Graziella.'

Fortuno seemed relieved to be away from the subject of love. The old men looked disappointed. 'And what about Molly?'

'Oh, Molly will probably have the time of her life in Rome before . . .' Before they snatch her back to Calne and the doggy sofas, regular church, no alcohol. 'Poor Molly.'

'Poor Molly indeed.' He sounded unsure whether he

215

was agreeing or deriding her misplaced sympathy. She looked at him properly, perhaps trying to gauge how far removed the kind, conscientious, serious Fortuno might be from this person who sat with her so restlessly, understandably upset at being thwarted in all his good intentions.

'Come,' and he stood up. 'Let's go home.'

'Cittavigile?'

'Where else?'

'But you said once . . .' She could not remember exactly what he had said. Besides, she felt she had used up all her conversational powers on the subject. To refute Cittavigile's suspicions she must live and die at the Villa Giulia, something she knew now she had always intended.

They passed the Fonte Maggiore and Fortuno took her arm. He said, as if with a conscious effort at throwing off his previous bad temper, his irritation at Molly, his anxiety that Nan would force him to make love to her at a café table, 'Father Emilio thinks you should marry again.'

'He's never said so to me.'

'He'd be too shy.'

'Father Emilio shy?'

A bell rang, on and on. Someone cried out in greeting far above, window to window perhaps. Nan could smell grilling peppers, drains. They were in a narrow street now and of necessity they walked like lovers, close, mutually protective.

'Anna,' Fortuno began.

'Don't tell me now,' she said. Between the buildings she could see the sunlight in the square ahead. It must be noon. Or later. With a small cry she looked at her watch.

'Look at the time!' and when Fortuno did so, his head close to hers, his expression exasperated, bewildered, tender, she added, smiling, because after all it had ceased to matter, 'We've forgotten Lily.'